withdrawn

LUSH

LUSH
NATASHA FRIEND

SCHOLASTIC PRESS • NEW YORK

Copyright © 2006 by Natasha Friend
All rights reserved. Published by Scholastic Press, an imprint of Scholastic Inc., *Publishers since 1920*. SCHOLASTIC, SCHOLASTIC PRESS, and associated logos are trademarks and/or registered trademarks of Scholastic Inc.

Library of Congress Cataloging-in-Publication Data

Friend, Natasha, 1972–
    Lush / Natasha Friend. — 1st ed.
        p.   cm.
    Summary: Unable to cope with her father's alcoholism, thirteen-year-old Sam corresponds with an older student, sharing her family problems and asking for advice.
    ISBN 0-439-85346-X (hardcover)
    [1. Alcoholism — Fiction.   2. Fathers — Fiction.   3. Family problems — Fiction.]
    I. Title.

PZ7.F91535Lu   2006
[Fic] — dc22
2005031333
12 11 10 9 8 7 6 5 4 3   6 7 8 9 10 11/0

Printed in the U.S.A.
First edition, October 2006

For B-Bear, my
third-trimester muse,
with love.

LUSH

CHAPTER ONE

Well, my father is at it again.

Saturday, 2:35 A.M., while all normal fathers are sleeping, mine stumbles through the door, breaks a vase, then proceeds to eat a plate of cold lasagna face-first.

From my post at the top of the stairs, I watch him. Still face-planting the lasagna. Still face-planting the lasagna.

If you ever catch your dad in this position, some advice: Flip on the light in the upstairs hall. Flip it off. Flip it on again. Do this until he finally lifts his head and squints around the kitchen — until you can see that he hasn't suffocated on ricotta cheese.

Later, when you are back in bed, listen for the uneven tread of his feet on the stairs. You will hear the clean thwack of some part of his body hitting something solid in the hall, and you will hear him swear.

"Ellie!" he will yell to your mother. He will stumble into their bedroom. "Ellen! Get the ice pack!"

Your mom will make her shushing sounds. "*Shhhhh.* Patrick. The kids."

And your dad will yell for her to get the ice, dammit. *Now.*

You know that your mother will do it. She always does.

In the morning there will be a bruise on your father's cheek. Or shin. Or elbow. But he won't remember how it got there. He won't remember a thing.

*　　*　　*

I don't know why my father drinks. Well, I kind of do. I asked him once and he said he does it for the snap.

"The snap," I repeated. I was picturing a pair of pants, tan with an elastic waist — the kind my little brother wears. But what my dad meant was entirely different. When he drinks, something in his brain snaps into place.

"Like how?" I asked.

"It's hard to explain," he said, and then he changed the subject to baseball. As if the Red Sox were more important.

"He's a good man," my mother said later, and I said, I know, I know, you tell me all the time.

"Samantha." My mother was irritated. "You'll understand when you're older."

"I doubt it," I said.

My mom doesn't get it, especially lately. Over the summer she went on a trip to California and while she was there she found yoga. Worse, she brought it home with her. Now she spends her day twisted up on the floor like a human pretzel, puffing through her nose.

My mother thinks she has the solution to everything: Just breathe through it. We joined this studio across town, a pink stucco monstrosity called the Yogi Palace. There's only one problem: My dad refuses to go. I don't exactly blame him. It is a place like nothing you have ever seen, full of freakshows. My mother says I will get used to it, like I got used to junior high. Aren't I happy there now?

"It's okay," I say.

People make a big deal about junior high, but the only thing I've noticed is you can't be friends with boys anymore. You get two choices: Either they are your enemies or they are trying to mash with you. There is no middle ground.

Take Charlie Parker, who lives three houses down from me and used to be my best friend. All through elementary school we spent our free time in the fort in his backyard, making up secret codes and planning spy attacks against the neighbors. Then seventh grade hit us, and what happened? The time capsule tragedy, where Charlie stole one of my bras and all the boys paid a buck to see it before it got buried. We haven't really spoken since, which stinks on so many levels. Level #1, Charlie Parker is the only person I ever told about my dad.

Once I was in the nurse's office at school and there was this pamphlet, *When Someone You Love Has a Drinking Problem.* I took the test, answering all twenty questions about you-know-who. I said yes to every single one.

"Would you like to take that with you?" the nurse asked.

I shook my head, put the pamphlet back in its cubby.

The nurse scooted her chair over next to me. She leaned in and placed the back of her hand on my forehead, soft as a butterfly. "What hurts?"

"Everything," I said. Then I waited to be told I didn't have a fever but I could take two Tylenol and be on my way. "Okay,"

I said. I actually walked out into the hall like I was going back to class. And then, when the nurse was busy in the supply closet, I snuck in and grabbed the pamphlet.

That is the worst part — the sneaking around. If your dad drinks, you hide it. Otherwise everyone will know and whisper about you behind your back. "We don't air our dirty laundry in public," my nana said once, when the subject came up. "Our business is our business. You want to talk about it, you come to me."

"I don't get that expression," I told her. "*Airing your dirty laundry.* Why would anyone want to smell our underwear?" But what Nana said stuck with me.

That is why I am careful about who I invite over to the house and when. My dad has to be long gone. He's an architect at a firm in town. Which means he is usually out of the house weekdays from seven A.M. to seven P.M., so I can have people over after school until dinner. No sleepovers, though. Weekends you just can't predict. I wonder sometimes what Angie and Vanessa and Tracey would think if they knew — if they saw my dad coming home after a good bender. I think they would run and hide in the closet, afraid that he might start throwing steak knives. I am waiting for something like that to happen myself.

So far it hasn't, but a person has to be prepared. The one thing I've learned is you just never know. One minute my dad is sitting quietly watching the ball game, drinking Jim Beam, the next he's slamming doors and swearing. I like it best when he's passed out on the couch under a blanket. His mouth is calm and soft. If I wanted to, I could put my hand on his chest, feel his heart beat, make sure he's okay.

Then sometimes I don't care if he ever wakes up.

It sounds confusing, I know. But when your father would rather drink than breathe, that's how it goes.

CHAPTER TWO

So I've written a note. I'm just waiting for the right person to give it to.

From the library stacks I survey the scene. In the corner, there is a table of high school boys, which everyone knows is the jock crowd — the hockey players. I like watching them, in a way. Especially the one in the green baseball cap. But that is not why I am here tonight. I am definitely looking for a girl.

There's a redhead by the windows. Pretty, but not too pretty. Her nose is funny and her hair is a mess, though not in that snob way like she's been riding around all day in a convertible — more like she has better things to do than brush it. Juliet, her name is. She carries an orange backpack with sayings all over it like *I Souport Publik Edekasion* and *A Woman Needs a Man Like a Fish Needs a Bicycle*, so you can tell she has a sense of humor. Overall she is the type that would know what to do in most situations and would give good advice, which is what I need.

I am holding the note in my palm. It is folded into the tiniest of squares, with a tab to pull open. I learned how to fold notes at camp. Also, how to hyperventilate, french, and use a tampon. So far, note folding is the only one I've mastered. I hope Juliet can read my writing.

Hi.

You may think it's nuts to write to a total stranger in the library but if you're the kind of person I think you are, you'll read this, anyway.

My name is Samantha. Sam. Here is the deal. First of all, my parents. They are a total mess. My dad is what you would call a big drinker (which really equals a big alcoholic — I have done my research). It is mostly whiskey but anything in a pinch. I worry about him and want to punch his lights out in the same second.

Then there's my mother, who is turning into a yoga freak right before our eyes. (No offense if you are one of those downward doggers, too, which I SERIOUSLY doubt, but if you are, I am sorry!) Anyway, she thinks breathing is the answer to everything and is just about driving me insane. They both are. The only person I can honestly say is not making me crazy is my brother, Luke, but he is only four so how much does that help?

There are other things I need advice on, such as boys and what to do with them, but this is not my #1 problem, just a question that is always with me.

I know what you're thinking: "Doesn't this girl Sam have any friends of her own to talk to?" And the answer is YES! I have lots. But they are all 8th grade girls like me and not experienced in the ways of the world (and don't even get me started on 8th grade boys, who are plain hopeless and occasionally evil). What I need is an older sister type, which is where you come in.

So my point is, if you ever have time between high school activities to tell me what you would do in my shoes, write back. I will check for a response note in 360.68TON, which is code for The History of Modern Whaling, this book that hasn't been checked out in 13 years. (This is my age exactly. Coincidence? I don't think so.) Anyway, I will check between pages 32 and 33 on Friday.

I think if you write back, you would be a big help and maybe I could be a help to you in some way, too. With baking tips, for example. That is something I am learning a lot about from this Muffins for Morons book my nana gave me for Christmas.

Well, thanks for listening. I will be looking for your reply. If you decide to, that is. No pressure or anything.

SAM

I wait until Miss Howe, the librarian, walks into the study room. "Boys and girls," she says in her pinchy voice, "the library will be closing in ten minutes."

I cup the note in both hands, shake it like dice. *Luck be a lady,* I think, remembering the song from a play I saw once. *Luck be a lady named Juliet.* And then I feel like a dingwad.

It is a stupid idea. Really, *really* dumb. Maybe the stupidest idea I have ever come up with.

I shake my head, put the note back in my pocket. Okay, then. I'm not going to do it. And because I'm not going to do it, I am saving myself from massive public library humiliation.

I leave the stacks, breezing past Juliet. I don't need Juliet. I can take care of myself, which I have been doing for thirteen years, thank you very much.

Breezing past the jock table is another matter. The last time I walked by, one of them said in his loudest whisper, "Nice rack." And another one said, "Sign me up, man."

I felt a little rush, but in it a little shame. I knew exactly what the words were referring to, and I knew they were shady compliments.

Sometimes, when I am in the bathroom at night, I lock the door. I stand in front of the mirror, lean in, and try to be objective. Someone other than me, looking at me.

Okay.

Nice-ish face, but nothing special. Green eyes. Small, straight nose. A few freckles. Teeth fine since the braces came off.

Hair: dirty blond, long. Wavy. Good, but not movie-star material.

Then I close my eyes and lift my shirt, breathe in deep through my nose. *In, in, in, in.*

It first came to my attention over the summer.

And ouuuuuuuut.

I went to bed with a flat chest and woke up with, well . . .

Open the eyes.

These.

I wasn't the one who noticed. It was my mom, at the beach, after I came running out of the water. The word "blossom" is one I don't care to hear again in this lifetime.

And the words "My, my, my. How old did you say you were, dear?" Which is what the department store lady said when she measured me for a bra.

From that moment on, I have made it a point to ignore my body. Clothes: the baggier, the better. Need to be naked? Lights out.

The only challenge so far has been the gym locker room, where everyone changes in front of each other. But all you have to do is pretend you're going to the bathroom. The stall can be your own personal dressing room.

As for the eighth-grade boys and their comments, I have my friends. Not exactly bodyguards, but close. Just having them with me — a withering gaze from Tracey here, a "shut up, dog breath" from Angie there — helps. Most of the time I don't even think about it.

Until now.

I know why the jock boys are staring at me, and I don't exactly mind. I even like it. Kind of. But it also freaks me out because, well, what next?

Outside, I look for my mother's car, the brown Toyota, ugly as sin. There it is, but my dad is driving, which makes my insides drop. Sometimes he is so cockeyed he can't even stay in his lane. Then I have to steer.

Now I am changing my mind about the whole note thing.

Back inside, the study room is empty. I leave the note on the fourth carrel from the left, Juliet's regular spot. Tomorrow it will be there for her, waiting.

*　　*　　*

Midnight, and I am having a snack at the kitchen table. It is cereal with whatever I can find for toppings: coconut, chocolate chips, grapes. The silence of the house wraps me like a quilt. The light from the street makes long shadows on the linoleum. It is spooky, but not.

At night, I eat however I want. No one is here to boss me. I can use my fingers, not use my napkin. And when I am done I can slurp the milk from the bowl.

I especially like flipping my head upside down and drinking from the other side, which always makes a mess on the floor. But so what?

Tonight my father appears out of nowhere. He has on his

striped bathrobe and one sock. His hair is everywhere. When he says hello, I jump.

"Trouble sleeping?" he asks.

I shrug. "Hungry."

"Ah." He is standing in the doorway, hands in his bathrobe pockets. There is a loop of yarn around his neck. It has pasta beads on it: macaroni, rigatoni, penne. Luke made it for him in preschool. I have one, too. We all do.

"I'm sorry," he says. "About tonight. I scared you."

"What makes you think that?" I ask.

I'm sassing him, I know. But he deserves it. On our way home from the library he hit a mailbox. I said he should let me drive, he wasn't safe. He looked at me like I had three heads. "You don't have a license," he said. And then, "I'm *okay.*" We made it home afterward, but I spent the whole ride in the crouch position, preparing for the worst.

"You can't drive when you're like that," I say, spoon raised for emphasis. "What if Luke was in the car?"

My father walks over and places both hands on my shoulders. "I know," he says. "I know, and I'm sorry. It won't happen again. You have my word."

My father's word. He gives his word like it's some precious jewel. He gives it, and then, when no one is looking, he steals it back. Once I heard him tell my mother, "Honey, I give you my word," and my mother said, "Well, your word is mud."

I can think of worse things than *mud* to describe my father's word.

"Did you tell Mom?" I ask. "About the car?" There is a dent on the right side now.

"Not yet. Tomorrow."

"Uh-huh."

"I can fix it with a toilet plunger," he says. "Did you know that?"

"No," I say, getting up from the table. "No, I did not."

"It's true. I'll show you in the morning."

"I have school in the morning."

My father nods. "Right. This weekend, then."

"Sure," I say. I believe that he means it, that he wants it to happen. And the truth is, I do, too.

When I was younger my dad didn't drink so much. We could have fun together. Once he took me to the zoo. In the monkey house we watched the apes and chimps. I rode on his shoulders, taller than everyone. He held my ankles so I wouldn't fall and we bounced up and down making jungle noises. Later we ate hot dogs with mustard, and ice cream with rainbow jimmies. My dad said I could have anything I wanted, anything at all, and I said, anything? He said, well, anything the zoo had to offer. I said, a giraffe! Can I have a giraffe? And he said if that's what you want, that's what we'll get. And I did get a giraffe that day — a stuffed one, but still.

"You going up?" my father says now.

I shrug. "I guess."

"Sammy."

"What."

"It won't happen again," he says. Unbelievably.

I look straight at his eyes. He means it so much it makes my heart hurt.

CHAPTER THREE

In the morning, my father skips breakfast. This is not new. What he tells us is he isn't hungry, he will grab a bagel at work. But I know the truth. He is hungover from drinking, too sick to eat.

"Where's Daddy?" Luke asks from his fort under the kitchen table.

I lift the tablecloth. "Daddy's at work. He left early."

"Great!"

Great! Sometimes you just have to look at Luke with amazement.

Our mother arrives, holding a platter. "Scrambled eggs, coming up."

But breakfast is not as simple as scrambled eggs. First there is the morning meditation. *Om, om, om. Shanti, shanti, shanti. Peace, peace, peace be to all.* It is not the words I object to. It is the singing. Why do we have to sing? Because, apparently, there's nothing the universe loves more than voices raised in song.

"How do you know what the universe loves?" I asked once.

"The teachings of the yoga sutra," my mother said, as if that explained it all.

"Well, who came up with it, then?" I asked. This was not to be fresh. I really wanted to know.

My mother frowned. "Don't be fresh, Sam." And that was the end of that.

Now she is back with more ways to complicate breakfast. Once we are seated, she starts in.

"*Surya namaskar,*" she says, spooning out eggs. "The sun salutation." And then, "Luke, take the straw out of your nose, please."

"Sorry, Mama!" Luke yells.

"Thank you, buddy." My mother sits down at the table, starts buttering toast.

I say, "If you stare directly at the sun, you go blind."

"Well," says my mother, a bite of toast in her mouth, "we're inside."

"The sun is a ball of fire," Luke says.

Mom nods. "That's right, Lukey. The sun *is* a ball of fire."

"That's right, Mukey," Luke says. "That's right, Bukey. That's right —"

"That's enough now," Mom tells him.

"Okay, Mama!"

"All right," she says. She takes another bite of toast, a swallow of tea. She is wearing a green fuzzy towel on her head, the latest in her turban collection.

"Mom?" I say.

"Yes?"

"Do we have to do this?"

"Yes!"

"What's the point?" Sometimes I cannot help myself. I have to step out onto that ice farther and farther, until I see cracks.

"Samantha," my mother says, halfway between annoyed and mad.

I say I am sorry and bow my head a little to mean it.

Mom sighs. "Quieting your mind is far from easy, Sam. The mind is like a playground, full of —"

"Let's go to the playground!" Luke yells.

I start to laugh, then think better of it. I put my hand on Luke's arm. "Let Mom finish."

My mother looks at me, kindness in her eyes. "Thank you, Sam."

"Yes." I sit back in my chair, palms to the sky, a good yogi.

"*Surya namaskar* . . ." Mom stops, clears her throat. Then she launches in. We will do the sun salutation each morning. We will use our warming breaths. Over time, our movements will become a graceful, smooth flow.

Oh, it is too hard not to ask. "What if they don't?" I want to know. "What if our movements are always jerky?"

My mother shakes her head, impatient. "It isn't about that."

"Okay," I say.

Mom takes a breath, long and slow, then lets it out through her nose. "Well. Let's try one, then. A practice one."

Luke goes ballistic. "Practice makes perfect! Practice makes perfect!"

If I didn't know better I would say Luke is playing his own game with our mother, trying to make her snap out of it. But Luke is only four. His words are so innocent, flying out of his mouth like birds. Crazy and free.

*   *   *

Once I get to school I can relax. Nobody mentions parents. Pretty much all anyone talks about is boys.

There is only one part of the day I can't stand, and that's gym class. First of all, my friends are in the other section, and second, the teacher is a drill sergeant. Based on my keen lack of athletic ability, Ms. Fish is always yelling at me. Today we are doing wind sprints because Ms. Fish loves nothing more than seeing us sweat bombs at nine in the morning.

I am running my hardest, but this is not good enough for Ms. Fish.

"Knees up, Frances!" she barks in my ear.

That is the other thing. She knows my name is Samantha Gwynn; it's right there on her clipboard. I've corrected her a dozen times. And yet —

"Frances!!! . . . Knees!!! . . . Up!!!"

"Should I keep going, Ms. Fish?" asks Molly Katz. She has finished her wind sprints and is jogging delicately in place.

"Good hustle," Ms. Fish tells her. "You can cool it down now."

"Are you sure?" Molly persists. "I'm not even tired."

This is classic Molly Katz. It is how she lets the whole world know she is a superior breed. The opposite of the rest of us.

*　　*　　*

Third period is Earth science, but I call it dirt science because all we have done so far this year is look at dirt. My lab partner is Jacob Mann, who is also dirty. Dirty fingernails, dirty ears, dirty mind. Every time I sit down, he takes it upon himself to make some boob comment. Either that or a blond joke.

The minute I pull out my chair he is ready for me. "Hey, Sam. How do you get a one-armed blond out of a tree?"

"I don't know," I say. "And I don't care."

Jacob makes his voice high and squeaky. "Wave."

"Hardy har har."

"I know, right?" Jacob snickers. "You blonds are wicked smart."

I rarely say anything back. Because I don't want to encourage him.

Here is the problem with eighth-grade boys, though: They don't need encouragement. They just keep on going, anyway.

*   *   *

At lunch I carry my brown bag across the cafeteria. I can see Angie waving. And Tracey. And Vanessa. They are all wearing button-down shirts (pastel) and jeans (dark washed). Also, barrettes (circa first grade). Last year short bangs were in, but this year everyone's hair is in that awkward stage of almost-grown-out.

I sit down and take out my ham-on-wheat.

"Now that we're all here," Angie says, "I have an announcement."

"You're getting a horse?" Tracey guesses.

Angie gives her a look. "I don't even *like* horses."

"You used to."

"Yeah. In, like, *fifth grade.*"

"Fine. What is it, then?"

"It's a boy," Angie says. Naturally. With Angie, announcements are almost always boy-related. "I've decided to go for Danny Harmon."

Vanessa stops blowing milk bubbles. She takes the straw out and licks it. "Um . . ."

"*Um* what?" Angie says.

"Well," says Vanessa, "I hate to be the one to tell you this, but . . ."

"*But?*"

"Okay," Vanessa says low. "Prepare your heart. . . . Danny Harmon . . . loves another." This is how Vanessa talks sometimes, straight out of a Harlequin romance. *Prepare your heart. Danny Harmon loves another.* She is in one of those book of the month clubs: twelve for $11.99 plus shipping. Every month a new book arrives, fat and shiny — some bare-chested man on the cover, riding a stallion, his hair all a-flow. Vanessa likes to compare the boys at school to the men in her novels. Jeremy Thatcher is like Lance from *Love Will Come Again.* Benji Cass could pass for Thorn's twin from *Pleasure Island.*

"Danny Harmon," Vanessa continues, "is in love with Molly Katz."

Angie shrugs. "So?"

"So," Vanessa says, "Molly Katz is beautiful. . . . No offense."

"Beauty is in the eye of the beholder," Tracey pipes in. "Handsome is as handsome does."

Angie sits back. "Thank you, Tracey. You are a true friend. When Danny and I get married, you will be a bridesmaid for sure."

Vanessa says, "Angie, I didn't mean —"

Angie holds up her hand. "I know you didn't mean to call me ugly. You will be a bridesmaid, too. So will Sam."

"Thanks," I say.

I have only been to one wedding in my life. It was my cousin Chrissy's and I was the flower girl. I had to wear a yellow dress with a lacy collar that itched. At the reception, my father got smashed. When he tried to dance with my mom, he fell down. The DJ had to help him up. Then my dad barfed on the gift table.

It's better when I don't think about it. I try not to. Mostly, when I am with my friends I forget — relax into the boy talk, into the now. Then, other times, my dad sticks in my head like a wad of gum.

CHAPTER FOUR

Quarter of five on Friday and the library is deserted. In the stacks it's showtime: Sam versus *The History of Modern Whaling*. "Open me!" the book says. But I won't do it right away. I always like the buildup to an event more than the event itself. Christmas Eve, not Christmas Day. Because who wants to be disappointed? You ask Santa for a cell phone; he brings socks.

I start by flipping to page one, squinting at the tiny print. It looks more like a book about ants than a book about whales. Then I turn the book over, inspect the back. Rings of white from the bottom of a milk glass. Miss Howe would have a hissy fit. Using a book as a coaster is a library felony. That and folding down page corners.

I hold the book in both hands, feel its heft. Did it weigh this much the last time I picked it up? Definitely not. There *must* be a note inside — a long one. On thick, cream-colored stationery. Blue ink. Script writing. No, not script — Juliet isn't the flowery type. Block letters, then. Neat.

Okay, I can't take the suspense anymore. I have to go to page 32, no matter if there's nothing there. No matter if all that's waiting for me is whales. Whales, whales, and more . . . well, what do you know? A piece of paper.

It is only loose-leaf, the school kind. And it's only folded in half, with a few scribbled-out math problems on the back.

To be honest, I am a little bummed with the presentation, but I forgive Juliet. All she must be used to is text messaging and e-mail. Someday I will teach Juliet a thing or two about the lost art of note writing. Like how you always use your best stationery, and how you should take the time to fold it in a special way. This shows you really care about the person. Once I spent three hours writing a note for my friend Lauren Weiner to read on the bus ride home from camp. Lauren called me that night to say a personal thank-you. Did I know how much better that note made her feel?

Yes. I know the impact of a good note, which is why I picked Juliet in the first place.

I sit on the carpet, unfold the paper, prepare to be wowed.

Muffins for Morons? Nana must think very highly of you. What's next, _Doughnuts for Dimwits?_

Well. This is not a good start.

If you want my advice, Samantha Sam, stop trying to fix your parents. You can't. The sooner you face facts, the better off you'll be.

A.J.K.

A.J.K.??? The note is plain rude, but I have bigger things to consider. Like who is A.J.K.?

The only person I can think of who might have found my note is the girl who's always sitting by Juliet, the one with the eyebrow ring. Only her name doesn't start with A. It's something with L. Lola? LeeLee?

I look around. There's no one in the library to spy on except Miss Howe, who is at the checkout desk, picking her teeth with a paper clip. You have to wonder what her first name is. Ruth, maybe. Or Enid. Yes, that's it. *Enid Howe.*

Miss Howe looks up and frowns. "The library will be closing in ten minutes."

Sure, Enid. Whatever you say.

*   *   *

Tonight I walk home. It's not far, and the streets are well lit and full of houses, which is the only reason my mother lets me go alone. I got the whole lecture when I was a kid: *Be aware of your surroundings at all times. Carry your house key in your hand. If a car stops and someone asks for directions, don't answer. Just keep walking. Run if you have to. Kick where it counts.*

All these warnings, and not just from my mom, either. From school and TV. It's like nobody trusts anyone, and I'm supposed to walk around scared all the time.

But I'm not scared, alone at night. I like the cool quiet.

When I turn onto Hamilton Street, I have to pass Charlie Parker's house to get to mine. He's in the driveway, playing basketball under the lights with his dad. Charlie's sister, Faye, is sitting in a lawn chair, styling her doll's hair with curlers. This is something I used to help her do, back when her jerk brother and I were still friends. And I don't even like dolls! I would just do it because Faye asked me to.

Now I want to cross the street more than anything, but that would be like letting Charlie Parker rule me. So instead I make myself keep going. I give Faye a little wave and hold my finger to my lips, hoping she will take the hint. She doesn't. "Hey, Sam!" she yells.

Mr. Parker turns around, palming the basketball. "Sam! Hey!" What he means is: "You're still alive? We haven't seen you in months, so we thought you kicked the bucket!" But I guess Charlie must have told him everything by now — *his* version of everything.

"Hey, Faye," I say. "Hey, Mr. P."

I keep walking down the sidewalk, adding a little bounce to my step. "Yo, Sam!" Charlie yells. "The silent treatment! Very original!"

No, it's the invisibility treatment. *The invisibility treatment,* you moron. I can feel my mouth wanting to scream the words, to prove how moronic he is. But then I would look just as bad.

"That girl has *issues,*" Charlie says to his dad. Loudly.

"Maybe her issue is *you,* hotshot," I hear Mr. Parker say. And I am reminded of what a good guy he is. Compared to his son. I walk faster, wishing so much Mr. Parker was my father. Wishing I didn't have to dread going home.

* * *

When I get there, my mother is on the living room floor, doing the plough pose. Her butt is in the air and she's puffing away.

"How was the library?" she asks between breaths. "Good time?"

"Good time since I *walked home*. Since I made it home *alive*."

Mom sits up. "Let's not get into that again," she says. "Daddy's sorry about the mailbox."

"It's not the mailbox I'm worried about."

"Sam."

"What? It could have been a *person*. A kid!"

"Your father told you, it won't happen again."

"Uh-huh."

My mother crosses her ankles over her knees. She pats the floor in front of her. "Come and sit with me. Try some warming breaths."

"I'm not in the mood to breathe right now."

I go to find Luke. He's busy on the couch, watching his Wiggles video. Every few seconds he jumps up, dances wildly, then flops back down.

"You're getting good," I say.

"Sammyyyy!" Luke jumps up, has a spaz.

"Lukey!"

"Wiggle with me!"

"Later, buddy. I've got homework. Boring stuff."

Luke wiggles his hips like a pro. You have to smile at him — you can't help it. His hair is sticking straight up. He's got egg on his shirt and a red juice mustache, and he couldn't care less.

I catch Luke in midair and hug him.

"Hey! Wiggle with me!"

Sometimes I wish I could jump up and down like a maniac next to my brother and forget my entire life. But I can't.

I put him down. "Later, Lukey."

I go to my room and lie on the bed. I take out A.J.K.'s pitiful excuse for a note and read it again. Who does A.J.K. think she is, anyway? Some kind of parent expert? What does A.J.K. know about anything, least of all me?

Outside, a car door slams. I wait until I hear my father's footsteps in the front hall. "Anyone home? . . . Ellie? Kids?" His voice sounds stumbly tonight. Which is not a good sign.

I go over to my desk and take out a piece of paper, my best stationery.

FIRST of all, my name isn't Samantha Sam. It's just Sam.

CHAPTER FIVE

On Saturday night my three best friends and I gather at Vanessa's house. Almost every weekend we sleep over because her basement is huge and her parents have the best snacks. Tonight it's ice-cream sundaes and popcorn, homemade by Vanessa's dad.

"I hope you girls like lots of butter," Mr. Barton says.

In the kitchen it's me, Vanessa, Angie, and Tracey, sitting at the butcher-block table in our nightshirts and slippers as we have been doing since third grade. Over the years, girls have come and gone around us. Danielle Thurlow moved to Colorado. Hannah March got cool in seventh grade and ditched us. Rachel Meyer. Sarah Tycz. But this group, this foursome, has stuck together. *Nice girls,* my mother calls us. *Good kids.* And we are. When I showed up tonight, everyone hugged me.

The best thing about Vanessa's house is that her parents leave us alone. As soon as the food hits the table, they head upstairs. "Don't stay up too late," Mrs. Barton says, but then she winks. She doesn't care what happens, as long as we stay in the house.

"So, do you think your parents are doing it right now?" Angie asks as we make our sundaes, sprinkling popcorn on top. We like to mix it up, weird combinations. Cookie batter and french fries. Oreo-Pringle sandwiches.

"Doing what?" says Vanessa.

"*You* know. . . . *It.*"

"What, sex?" Tracey makes a face. "Ew."

"*Making love* is what you should call it," Vanessa says. "And, yes, they probably are."

"Could we *please* change the subject?" Tracey says.

Angie laughs. "You think your parents don't do it? How do you think you got here? Immaculate conception?"

When we were in sixth grade, Angie's sister Marybeth gave us The Talk. We sat on an old picnic blanket in the Martinellis' attic. No one said a word except for Marybeth. "And then, the guy puts his thing in the woman's thing," she explained. "A bunch of white stuff squirts out, and *voilà*! Bun in the oven."

"I know how I got here," Tracey says, punching Angie in the arm. "I just don't want to *discuss* it."

That's about as far as things go. A little talk around the edges of sex. There is so much I still wonder about, but how is a person supposed to bring it up? Once when I was ten, I walked in on my parents kissing in the pantry, my dad's hand on the small of my mother's back. I was embarrassed, but also relieved. The day before had been a bad drinking day, full of yelling. I didn't think they would ever make up, but somehow they did.

"How's Danny Harmon?" Vanessa asks.

"Danny Harmon," Angie says, "is my one true love."

"Yeah," Tracey says. "Tell us something we don't know."

Vanessa reaches into her backpack and pulls out a book. *Gabrielle's Wish.* "Speaking of true love, you know how Loren and Gabrielle found out they were brother and sister and their love could never be? We were like, 'No way. That's so gross.' Well, guess what. . . . Gabrielle was adopted! They're free to love after all!"

"Oh, goody," Angie says. "Now I can sleep at night."

Vanessa punches Angie in the arm.

"Hey! What's with all the violence?"

Tracey says, "We can't help it. You're so punchable."

"Shut up and pass the hot fudge," Angie says.

Vanessa shakes her head. "It's not hot anymore."

"Shut up and pass the cold fudge."

I laugh along with everyone. I'm just glad I'm not at home. I would rather be here, in this kitchen, with parents who love each other upstairs.

*   *   *

When I get home, the first thing I do is check on Luke.

"How was Daddy last night?" I ask.

"Daddy!" Luke says, bouncing on the bed. "Was loud!"

I stand in front of him, in case he goes flying.

"Loud how?" I ask. "Banging around? Or yelling? Or what?"

Luke tosses a pillow in the air. "You got it!"

This is how a conversation with Luke goes.

"Which one, Luke? Was Daddy yelling?"

A stuffed bear hits the ceiling. "Yessiree!"

"Sit down with me," I say. "Stop bouncing for a minute and sit. Please." I'm getting that pit in my stomach now, the one that comes on Sunday mornings. I should have stayed home last night.

"No sitting!" Luke yells. "Bouncing!"

He seems okay, my brother. The same as always.

"Don't bounce too high, buddy," I tell him. "Be careful."

* * *

My mother and father are in the living room. I stand in the doorway for a minute, watching. My mom pulls a blanket over my dad and takes off his shoes. There's a hole in one of his socks, and the big toe sticks out.

"Mom?" I say, not bothering to whisper. When my dad is passed out, a marching band could be in the room and he wouldn't blink an eye.

"*Shhhh,*" she says, and gestures to the door.

In the kitchen, we sit facing each other.

"He's just exhausted, Sammy," my mother says. "He's been putting in such long hours at work."

I don't say anything, and she sighs, as if to say, *What?*

"I'm not *stupid*, Mom."

"I know you're not."

"Do you?"

My mother picks up a place mat, flips it over. "There's a lot going on that you don't know about, Sam."

"So tell me."

"It's complicated. Your dad's under a lot of pressure right now and he needs our support."

"What about what *we* need?"

30

Mom holds her palms up to the ceiling. "What am I supposed to do, Sam?"

I shrug. "You're the parent. You tell me."

* * *

Bedtime, and my father is in my room. As usual, I have to wonder why he bothers to show up at all. He is so far removed from what is going on in my life that he probably doesn't even know what grade I'm in. He stands in the doorway, fiddling with his earlobe, and I just stare at him. Part of me wants him to come and sit next to me on the bed and smooth my hair with his big, warm hand. The other part wants to shove him over backwards. When he says goodnight, I just nod.

Once I heard my father talking about me, in my parents' bedroom at night. "She's growing up too fast," he said. "I want to slow her down."

"You can't hold on too tight," my mother said. "You have to let her find her way."

Tonight I kind of wish my dad *would* hold on too tight, just to show me he still feels that way. But if he tried to hug me I'd be mad. Standing in the doorway and saying goodnight is probably all he can think of to do. And it's not enough.

CHAPTER SIX

When Charlie Parker passes me in the hallway, I ignore him some more.

He and his so-called friends are all wearing jeans halfway down their butts so their boxers show. The sad thing is, they think it looks good.

"Hey, Parker," Kyle Faulkner says. "There's your girrrrl-friend."

I stare into my locker, concentrate on the microscopic piece of tape on my English binder.

"In your dreams," I hear Charlie say. Which makes absolutely no sense.

Then come the usual comments, all boob-related, mostly out of Greg Vaughn's mouth. There's a lot of laughter, and I personally can't tell if Charlie is a part of it or not, but as far as I'm concerned he is already guilty.

Don't look, I tell myself. *He's not worth it.* But then I think, *Yes, look. He deserves to be glared at.*

I whip around, but all I see is Charlie Parker's back. He and his posse are entering the science room. Then, at the very last second, he turns to look at me.

I mean to shoot him the bird. Or, at least, the hairy eyeball.

But instead I find myself sticking out my tongue. Like a third grader. Which is horrifying. I have no idea what made me do it, yet here I am.

Charlie raises an eyebrow at me, cool and slow.

I want to scream at him. I try to. But somehow, amazingly, my tongue is still out.

*   *   *

The library is packed. The jock table is a sea of sweatshirts. Walking by, I hold my breath. The boy in the green baseball cap looks up and smiles at me, and when he does I can feel a little zing up my spine.

Miss Howe is making the rounds, holding a finger to her lips. I work my way to the stacks. The reshelving guy is there, lumbering around with his weird hair and ugly shoes, but I don't let that stop me.

I slide *The History of Modern Whaling* off the shelf, holding it in my lap for a minute. When I get to page 32 a scrap of paper is waiting. Yellow. Raggedy. It is ugly looking, but I don't care. Relief is flooding my insides, making me breathe again.

Just Sam,

You've got to learn to lighten up or you'll never make it in high school. It gets a lot worse than dimwit comments, trust me. That's too bad about your dad. Look on the bright side — at least he isn't forcing you to be the next David Beckham when you'd rather play Ado Annie opposite Tom Lombardo in the school play.

A.J.K.

Well, what did I expect — a miracle?

I peer around the stacks at the study room. The jock boys are all laughing hysterically, probably at one of those silent-but-deadly farts they are so fond of. Juliet and her friend with the eyebrow ring are quizzing each other off flashcards. On the couch a few girls are piled on top of each other reading *Elle*. No one is watching me.

A.J.K.?

Is it the girl with the long black braid? The one with the fuzzy boots and army pants? The blond whose hair looks like a shampoo commercial? Please, don't let it be her.

Part of me wants to know who it is. But then there's the nervous-excited feeling of not knowing that I want to hold on to for a while.

While no one is looking, I whip out a piece of paper.

A.J.K.

Isn't David Beckham that soccer guy with the anorexic wife??? Explain. And while you're at it, who is this Tom Lombardo character? Is this just a play you want to be in or are

we talking about a big-time crush
here?

SAM

P.S. My dad thinks he's being sneaky
when he tries to hide his bottles but
yesterday I found one — guess where.
Behind the toilet!!! He can't even go to
the john without having a drink and
that makes me want to hurl.

P.P.S. About the A.J.K. thing. Can you
at least tell me what one of the letters
is for?

When I get home, Nana is in the kitchen making tea. She's
my dad's mom, Nana Gwynn, and she lives all the way in
Newburyport, so I am surprised to see her. The last time she
showed up unannounced was the time my dad went missing,
when I was in seventh grade.

I remember the whole scene — being squooshed on the
couch between Nana and Mom while a police officer peppered
us with questions. Detective Shultz, his name was, with a bushy
mustache and slicked-back hair.

"When did you last see your husband, Mrs. Gwynn?"

Just like a detective on TV would say.

"What was he wearing? Does he have any distinguishing characteristics?"

All the while jotting things down in a tiny notebook.

It took the police three days to find my dad, and when they finally dropped him off, he was covered in mud and smelled like barf. I had to hold my breath when I hugged him.

Nana's smell is the opposite. Cherry throat drops and cinnamon.

"Let me look at you," Nana says, stepping back. "... My word!"

"I know," I say. "Five foot four now."

Nana makes clicking noises with her tongue and shakes her head like she can't believe it. "The breast fairy made a visit."

Oh. My. God. If there were a hole in the floor right now, I would crawl in.

Nana smiles. "It's a blessing.... Women would give up their firstborn for ta-tas like those."

Well. How is a person supposed to respond?

"Yeah," I say, looking around the kitchen. "My father took off again, didn't he?"

"Let's not jump to conclusions," Nana says lightly. She pats my hand in that grandmotherly way and pours more water into her teacup. She is wearing a peach velour sweat suit, nude socks, and heels. She is the thinnest person I know, and her eye shadow goes all the way up to her eyebrows, a rainbow of browns. My mother doesn't wear any makeup. She is into the natural look. Not Nana. Every time she takes a sip of tea, lipstick stays on the cup, a peachy smear.

"So," Nana says, "how are the boys?"

I stare at her blankly. "Dad and Luke?"

Nana smiles. "The boys at school."

Ah. *The boys at school.* The bra-snappers who smell like gym socks and can burp the alphabet? The ones who stare at my chest on a daily basis and say things like, "Hey, Sam, is it cold in here or are you just glad to see me?"

I manage to nod politely. "They're okay."

"How about the boy down the street? With the curls."

"Charlie Parker."

"That's the one. How's Charlie Parker?"

Besides being the world's biggest jerk? "He's okay."

"I'll bet he is." Nana winks like we're sharing a little secret, just the two of us.

"Uh-huh," I say. "So. My dad is home right now?"

Nana pauses to take a sip of tea. "Not yet," she says. "Your mom's out . . . picking him up." More tea sipping. "I'm sure they'll be back soon."

"Sure," I say. I know what this means. My mom is out driving around looking for my dad — checking all the bars, and the parks, too. *Back soon* could be three minutes or three hours. Or three days.

"Don't worry," Nana says.

I can feel the familiar tightening in my belly, but I look Nana straight in the eye.

"Why would I worry?" I say.

*   *   *

I am upstairs, locked in the bathroom. I am standing in front of the mirror with my pajama top yanked up, staring. *Women would give up their firstborn for ta-tas like those.* Super.

Oh, I am missing my kid self so much right now. Young and flat and clueless about everything from boys to the whiskey bottle behind the toilet. Sometimes I wish I could say to six-year-old Sam, "You had it so good. And you didn't even know it."

* * *

Three A.M., and my parents are home. The minute the front door opens I jump out of bed. I crouch at the top of the stairs, where I can hear everything.

My mom is crying pretty hard. "Why?" she says, over and over again. "Why do you keep doing this?"

My father is slumped against the wall, holding his head. "I don't know," he says each time she asks why. *I don't know, I don't know, I don't know.*

My mom wants my dad to go to something for alcoholics — a place called *A.A.* — but he says no. He's not an alcoholic, he tells her. He knows he drinks too much and he's going to cut back — way back. This was a real wake-up call, what happened tonight. There are going to be some changes around here. Big changes.

Okay, I know I'm supposed to feel better hearing this. But I don't. It sounds like the same old speech with different words. *Big changes. I promise. Trust me. You have my word.*

The only thing that makes me feel better is going to see Luke. Right now he's curled up in bed, wearing his railroad pajamas, a teddy bear tucked under one arm like a purse. I watch him sleep and think how lucky he is that he doesn't know anything yet.

I lie down next to my brother and bury my nose in his neck. He smells so good, like baby shampoo and milk. I want him to smell this way forever.

CHAPTER SEVEN

In the morning my father walks downstairs and sits at the kitchen table. He asks, "What's for breakfast?" as though he is a normal person.

"Um. Hello?" I say. There's a pile of pancakes in the middle of the table, as high as the Hancock Building. And syrup and butter. What is he, plastered?

Nana smiles. She pats his cheek like he is a kid. "Blueberry pancakes. Fresh from the griddle."

"Ah," my dad says. "My favorite."

Luke goes ape. "Mine, too, Daddy! Mine, too!"

I watch the three of them and shake my head. Then my mom jumps into the act and kisses his cheek. "Good morning, honey! Sleep well?" Chipper as can be in her orange turban.

All I want to do is yell out, *What are you people, BLIND???* My father made it home alive, and I'm glad. But just because he's eating pancakes doesn't mean he's different. It doesn't mean he's fixed.

A.J.K.

You know where my mom found my dad?
Passed out under that bridge in Cross

Park where all the bums and druggies
go. (If you think I'm making this up you
can just think again.) He has a big bump
on his head, too, that of course nobody
knows how he got. How do I get this
information, you ask? Well, I'll tell you,
it's not easy. I have to spy at the top
of the stairs with my bionic ears.

This morning we are all supposed to
be so happy that he's home that we
"forgive and forget," as my mom says,
which if you ask me is only one notch
better than "just breathe through it."
I, for one, don't forget a thing. I just
sit around waiting for something worse.

SAM

I go to school mad. The last place I want to be is gym class
with Ms. Fish. Today she puts us into pairs and gives us a
medicine ball that weighs as much as Luke. Next to wind
sprints, this is Ms. Fish's favorite torture technique: strength
training. We are told to throw chest passes while side-squatting
across the gym. Every other squat we are supposed to drop
and do a push-up.

Right.

My partner is Marsha Fine, captain of the field hockey
team. She has hands the size of a grown man's and legs carved
from granite.

"Try to keep your feet facing the same direction," Marsha says between chest passes. "And your knees bent. Like this. See?"

Not really.

"Do you mind if we pick up the pace a little? I'd like to get my heart rate up."

You do that.

"Hey, Samantha. Why are you stopping? We're supposed to go to the end of the gym."

I give Marsha a shrug, which is kind of like a *who cares.*

"Suit yourself."

I make myself comfortable on the floor, which Marsha doesn't seem to mind. She keeps right on side-squatting and push-uping without me, tossing the ball in the air to herself. She is all about the workout.

"On your feet, Frances!"

Oh, I would love so much to spit on Ms. Fish's sneakers right now, but it would take too much effort.

"I don't feel well," I say.

Ms. Fish frowns. "What hurts?"

"I don't know."

"You don't *know?*"

I shrug. Right now, I don't care if Ms. Fish yells at me. I just want to sit here for the rest of the day. Maybe the night, too.

"I don't know," I mumble.

"I see."

Everyone in the gym is looking at me now. I can hear Molly Katz and her friends giggling.

"It just feels better sitting down."

"Then it will just feel better taking a zero for the rest of the week," Ms. Fish says in a low, hard voice. "Is that what you want?"

"Yes," I say. "Yes, it is."

Ms. Fish turns away from me, disgusted. She blows her whistle to signal the end of class, and all the girls rush into the locker room.

I stay where I am. I recline on the shiny floor and close my eyes, thinking about breakfast. The funny thing is, I don't remember my father eating a single bite of blueberry pancake. I remember a big untouched pile on his plate. I remember him saying, "Ah. My favorite," which I now hear as a pure lie. Because his favorite is liquid. The opposite of food.

*   *   *

I am still mad in math class, but I am coming out of it. I like Mr. Hunt, the algebra teacher. Mr. Hunt doesn't require medicine balls. He has a calm, soothing voice. Plus, he lets us work with anyone we want.

Angie hates math, so my job is to help her through the pain. "Think of it as a little puzzle," I tell her.

"I hate puzzles," Angie says. "You know that."

"Come on," I say. "Let's start with an easy one. *Two x squared equals pi.*"

Angie raises an eyebrow. "*Three z triangled equals chocolate pudding.*"

*   *   *

I am almost to the library. Tonight it looks warm all over, lit up like a Christmas tree against the dark sky. On the front steps, a group of high school girls gathers, giggling, heads close together. Friends. Sometimes I wish Angie and V. and Tracey lived closer, so they could come with me. But they live on the other side of town, nearer to the West Branch Library. Besides, part of me likes coming here alone, keeping it mine.

I climb the steps, and the high school girls look me up and down. I know that look. It is the same one some of the girls at my school give, especially Molly Katz and that crowd — always on the lookout for another girl's flaws. Waiting for her to leave so they can whisper behind her back.

Well, let them whisper. Who really cares?

I walk by the front desk, past Miss Howe, who peers at me over the top of her glasses. It takes a lot to get Miss Howe to smile. In all the times I've been to the library I've only seen it happen once. It was when a handsome grandfatherly type complimented her sweater. That's the only time. Well, I might be the same way if my job was to make a bunch of teenagers be quiet every second.

Right now I can hear them, and that's from two rooms away. I know the boy in the green baseball cap is in there. I can picture him sitting in his usual spot, with his books spread out in front of him and a pencil tucked behind one ear.

Walking by the jock table, I can feel eyes on me. If I turn to look, Green Cap Boy will smile — but I can't get up the nerve to do it. So I keep on walking.

In the 300's, I crouch with *The History of Modern Whaling* on the floor in front of me. After a second I can tell I'm not alone.

"Excuse me."

I look up.

Ugly shoes, weird hair.

Great.

But the shelving guy doesn't seem to notice what I'm doing. He just wheels his cart on by, eyes to the ground.

Eeyore. That's who he reminds me of. Eeyore from *Winnie-the-Pooh.* Whenever I see the shelving guy, he looks the same way. Run over.

Come on, I want to say. *It can't be that bad.*

And then I think, well, maybe it is. What do I know?

Anyway, I can't get caught up in depressed donkeys right now. There's reading to be done.

Okay, Just Sam.

If you really want to play the My Father Is Worse Than Your Father game, the first thing you need to know is this: Not only does my dad hate who I am but he wants me to be just like him. And if I can't change, I'll tell you this much: He will not want to be related to me. End of story.

So here is what I do. I pretend I am the person he wants me to be, while inside I am dying a little bit more each day. He's not a malicious person — I'm not saying that — he's just judgmental as hell. And he has a vision for my future that does not exactly include show tunes.

As for Tom Lombardo, he will just have to

remain the object of my very, very distant affection. Trust me when I tell you that I am not his type. I'm not going to explain why right now, you're going to have to take my word for it. (Sorry, did I sound like YOUR father there? Hardly har.)

Well, I think that's enough of the A.J.K. autobiography for the time being, unless you want to hear about my mother and her latest get-rich-quick scheme, or my brother, Peter, and how he can do no wrong. . . .

Nah. I think I will spare you the gory details.

The "J" is for Jessup. My mother's maiden name. Argh. Why are parents allowed to name us without our permission?

A.J.K.

I pocket A.J.K.'s note and take a pen out of my backpack.

What's so bad about Jessup? I like it.
At least it's original. My middle name is
Jane. Could my parents be any lamer?

After I put my note safely in the whaling book I peek through the stacks at the jock table — the usual sweatshirts. But no green baseball cap. Perhaps a certain someone had to go to the bathroom.

Hmmm. Suddenly I feel courage. Also, the urge to pee.

I take the long way out of the stacks, avoiding the study

room altogether. Outside the bathroom I stop at the water fountain for a drink. When I stand up, someone's hands are over my eyes.

The old Guess Who game. Angie and V. and Tracey and I play it all the time. Only they're not at the library.

"Guess who," the voice says. A guy voice.

I shake my head. "I need a hint."

A deep laugh in my ear. "I think you know."

My face is hot. "Romeo Montague?"

More laughter. Good reaction.

"You're Samantha, right?"

I smile. "Nope." *You know my name?* I want to say. But don't.

He is so close I can feel the warmth of him. I can smell his skin. It reminds me of camp, woodsy and sharp.

"What do you say, Samantha?" he asks. "Should I take my hands off yet?"

Suddenly I'm shy. Shy and thirteen years old. I have no business standing here with a high school boy. I know from Angie's sister Marybeth that high school boys are only looking for one thing. And that's not a study buddy.

The hands are off and I spin around. Green Cap Boy, in the flesh. Green Cap Boy, holding me thisclose.

"I'm Drew."

"I'm Sam."

"I know," he says. And his eyes are so blue and his teeth are so white that I do the only thing I can think of. I bolt.

*   *   *

47

At home, Nana is in the kitchen, baking cookies.

"How was the library?" she asks. "Did you find what you were looking for?"

"Uh-huh," I say. It is easier than telling the real story. *So first I put this note revealing all our family secrets in this book about whales, and then this high school boy I don't even know practically felt me up, and then . . . I ran.*

Now Nana starts in with her dirty laundry routine. I didn't mention my dad's night to anyone, did I? I didn't say anything to my friends, right? Because, really, it's none of their concern. It's family business. I understand that, don't I?

"I didn't tell anyone," I say.

Nana sighs and pats me on the arm with an oven mitt. "You're a good girl, Samantha."

I look at her. Would I be a *bad* girl if I talked to my friends?

"Your father loves you very much," Nana says.

I nod, reach for a cookie. Oatmeal, Nana's specialty.

"He's just fine now, honey," Nana says. "You know that, right?"

Right.

CHAPTER EIGHT

In the morning my father has an announcement. There've been some changes at work, he tells us, and guess what? He's being promoted! He's going to head up the Feingold project!

"Oh, Paddy," Nana says, smiling like her face might break in half.

"Great!" Luke says. Then, "What's bine goad?"

My dad explains that the Feingold building will be one of the biggest, most elaborate constructions in the city. An architect's dream, he tells us. And he's in charge!

"Your dad is in charge!" my mother repeats, as though we're morons.

And the whole while, I am thinking, *How? How on Earth is this possible?* But then I realize that no one at the office knows my father spent Friday night passed out in a cardboard box.

I try to picture him in a work setting, clean and neat and smelling minty fresh — the opposite of his Sunday-morning smell. What is he like? Does he smile and make small talk as he walks into the office? *Mornin', Margaret. Cold enough for ya?* Is he clever and charming in meetings, impressing people with his big ideas and square jaw? I don't know this version of my dad, this Patrick Gwynn, Hotshot Architect.

If he's so great at work, why can't he be that great at home?

"Sammy?"

My mother is looking at me. They all are.

"What?"

"Aren't you going to congratulate Daddy?"

I look in my father's direction, focus on the light switch over his left shoulder. "Congratulations," I say.

*   *   *

After breakfast, Nana says good-bye. Now that my dad is one hundred percent wonderful again, she can go home. Her job is done.

Part of me is glad she's leaving. Farewell, denture cream, and liver for dinner, and endless, endless questions. The other part is nervous. What if everything goes to crap after Nana leaves?

We all stand on the porch. From the look on my mother's face, I can tell she's not so sure about Nana leaving, either.

"You don't have to go yet, Jean," my mom says. "Stay another night or two."

Nana shakes her head. "It's time."

When Nana moves in for a hug, I hold on tight and breathe in her cookie smell. "Love you," Nana says low in my ear.

"Love you, too," I say, and am surprised to feel the hot rush of tears in my eyes. As soon as Nana lets go, I bend down and pretend to tie my shoe.

My father asks Nana if she has enough gas in the car. Change for the toll?

"'Nuff gas?" Luke says. "'Nuff change?"

Nana kisses the top of Luke's head. "More than enough."

Then she turns to my dad. "Walk an old lady to her car?"

"But of course," he says, lifting a suitcase with one arm and holding out the other to Nana, like she is the queen of England.

If you watch the two of them standing in the driveway, facing each other, you don't need to be a professional scriptwriter to know how the conversation goes.

Nana:	*Don't scare us like that again, Paddy, you hear?*
Dad:	*I won't.*
Nana:	*No more disappearing acts?*
Dad:	*Not a one.*
Nana:	*How do I know?*
Dad:	*I give you my word.*
Nana:	*And you'll cut back on the drinking?*
Dad:	*Yes. Absolutely.*
Nana:	*Cross your heart?*
Dad:	*And hope to die, stick a needle in my eye.*

The way the scene ends is with Dad giving Nana the world's toothiest smile and the world's strongest hug, and with Nana driving off down the street, tooting her horn.

Cool as a cucumber.

Happy as a clam.

Because he told her what she wanted to hear.

* * *

It's the first Wednesday of the month, which means eighth-grade assembly. So far this year we've had to suffer through

How to Build Study Skills, How to Become a Better Citizen, and How to Communicate Effectively with Teachers. On each of the last three feedback forms, I wrote the same thing: *Bored nearly to death.*

Molly Katz, who is not only gorgeous but also student council president, stands onstage in a minidress.

"Her legs are orange," Angie whispers. "Self-tanner much?"

"Jealous much?" I whisper back.

"Oh, yes. I really want skin the color of carrots."

I try to frown disapprovingly at Angie but end up giggling instead. This is the power of Angie: She's so funny you forget she's mean.

"Good morning, eighth graders," says Molly Katz, holding the microphone to her shiny pink lips.

"Good morning, Molly!" says the entire auditorium, Angie included.

This is the power of Molly Katz. Even though you don't want to be riveted by her, you can't help yourself.

"Today, we are honored to have with us Doctor Monica Garner, who will be presenting on the topic of intimate relations."

I feel Angie's elbow in my ribs.

"This is *it*," Angie says.

"This is *what?*"

"Intimate relations. The *sex* assembly."

Ah. The sex assembly. Marybeth told us about it back in sixth grade. And now, here it is at last.

Angie makes an obscene pelvic gesture in her seat. I laugh out loud.

Suddenly, boredom is no longer an option.

*　　*　　*

At lunch, it's all anyone can talk about.

"Boys have it worse," Tracey says. "Definitely."

"What?" Vanessa says. "The whole appendage-sticking-out-when-you-least-expect-it thing?"

"Yeah. Like in the middle of *class* even. In *front* of everyone. . . . You couldn't pay me enough money to be a boy."

"Are you kidding me?" Angie says. "What about childbirth?"

"And periods," I add.

Angie shakes her head. "Forget that. My mother says giving birth is like pooping out a watermelon."

"Gross!" Tracey says.

I put down my sandwich. "Seriously, Angie. We're eating."

"Okay," Angie says, holding up a pencil. "I'm just saying. Hole the size of an eraser. Head the size of . . . what? Tracey's backpack?"

Tracey widens her eyes, shakes her head in horror. "I'm never wearing that thing again!"

Just before the bell rings, Kyle Faulkner and Greg Vaughn get up and prance by our table, oranges under their shirts.

"Who am I?" Kyle Faulkner asks, cupping his chest.

Greg Vaughn follows, one orange slightly higher than the other. "Who am I?"

I shake my head, almost imperceptibly. The fruit-as-boobs act is not new. But today, they're looking straight at me.

So is every other boy in the cafeteria, Charlie Parker included. When I catch him looking, he turns away. Coward.

Within seconds Angie, Vanessa, and Tracey go commando.

They make their eyes squinty-mean, they hiss, they hurl mini carrots. The lunch monitor sees them and threatens to call in the principal.

"We're uncomfortable dining in this environment," Angie says.

Vanessa nods. "It's sexual harassment."

Pretty soon the monitor backs down. The bell rings and lunch is over.

On our way to class Angie throws an arm around me. "Imbeciles," she says. "Imbeciles with hormones."

*　　*　　*

As annoying as the eighth-grade boys and their stupid boob fruit are, I am not thinking of them as I walk home from school. I am not thinking about Charlie Parker. I am not thinking about my dad.

I am thinking about Drew.

I replay the scene by the water fountain over and over again. I think, what if I didn't run? Would he have kissed me? And if he did, what would the kiss be like? Soft and sweet, or wet and wild like in the movies? Would he think I was a bad kisser? What if when he kissed me my breath smelled like pickles?

And what about that hand just below my bra? Was he trying to do what I think he was trying to do?

This thought makes me a little dizzy.

For a second, I allow myself to imagine something beyond kissing — something I have never done before — and what I see doesn't look entirely disgusting.

CHAPTER NINE

On Saturday morning, another bombshell. My father has decided to give yoga a shot. He's got on the stretchy pants and everything.

"You've *got* to be kidding me," I say. I turn to my mother. "He's kidding. Right?"

"Daddy is turning over a new leaf," she says, and you can tell she is feeling like the champion of the world right now.

"Great," I say, meaning the polar opposite.

"Great!" Luke yells. Meaning, *Great!*

My dad slings a gym bag over one shoulder. "And afterward, we'll go to Houlihan's for lunch. As a family."

I don't know what bothers me more, the sight of my father in spandex or the words coming out of his mouth. Who does he think he is, Father of the Year all of a sudden?

"Last time I went there," I say, "I found a worm in my hamburger."

My mother gives me a look.

"What? It's *true*. I ate a worm burger. I almost hurled."

Luke thinks this is the funniest thing he's ever heard. He actually rolls around on the floor clutching his belly. "Worm burger!"

"Wherever you want, then," my father says. "You choose. Okay?"

He is looking at me, his eyes pleading a little.

"Whatever," I say. My voice is a knife, and I know my father can feel it, and I don't care.

* * *

Yoga is a nightmare. It's me, my mother, and my father in a sweat box full of heavy breathers and the world's supply of body hair.

Luke, down the hall in the Baby Om room, gets to dance, and pretend to be a starfish, and practice blowing up balloons. He is in heaven.

Meanwhile I am being tortured. One breath at a time.

"Close right nostril. In, left nostril."

The yogi's name is Ajith. A tiny Indian man in an all-white outfit, with long brown fingers and feet that grip the floor like Spider-Man.

"Close left nostril. Out, right nostril."

Every Saturday since August, I have been coming here with my mother, covering one nostril and breathing through the other, then switching. Then switching again. And every Saturday I have done it, because it makes my mom happy. I haven't even fought it, really.

But now my dad is here, sitting on the mat next to me. Sucking up the same air.

"In, both nostril. Hold breath."

Sideways, I watch him.

"Out, both nostril."

My father is doing everything Ajith says. Breathing, holding, breathing. He doesn't seem relaxed, though. His shoulders are too hunched. His legs don't bend right. He looks too big for his mat.

"Now. Rub hands. Make heat."

I actually don't mind this part. It's like rubbing two sticks together to make a spark.

"Cover eyes."

I can feel my fingertips, warm against my eyelids. It is an odd sensation, but a comforting one, too. When I am in bed at night, I do this sometimes. Not the breathing bit, but the fingers on the eyes. Because sometimes I need tricks to fall asleep.

Here, at the Yogi Palace, I am wide awake. I can't focus on my breathing. I can only focus on my dad. And it makes me want to scream.

"Stand up tall. Like tree. Fingers long . . . longer."

Ajith is next to me now, his touch light on my arms. Lifting, lifting. He wants me to leave everything heavy behind. Reach, reach, reach. Up, up, up.

But Ajith doesn't know it all. He doesn't know me. And right now I don't want to be a tree. I want to get out of here, fast.

If I don't, my father is going to get a gigantic shove in the back, and he's going to hit the floor hard.

"I have to pee," I whisper to my mother. I walk out into the hall, where the air is cool and fresh. Where I can breathe.

* * *

Lunch as a family means sitting in a booth facing my father, who asks questions a dad should already know the answers to, like what's new in school and how are your friends. I keep my answers as short as humanly possible. *Fine. No. No. No. Uh-huh.*

The waitress comes to take our order.

"What do you have on tap?" my father asks. Then, "I'll have a Corona." To my mother he says, "Give me a break, Ellen. It's just one beer."

Mom puts on a smile that looks like it belongs on somebody else's face. To the waitress she says, "I'll have the Cobb salad and an iced tea, please. With lemon."

I order french fries, a Coke, and a hot butterscotch sundae with nuts, just daring my mother to stop me.

If Dad can order whatever he wants, I will say, *why the hell can't I?*

But my mother doesn't say a word. By the time the food comes, I have lost my appetite.

* * *

Later I sit on the porch swing, reading. It's one of those surprisingly warm fall afternoons where everyone is outside saying to each other, "Can you believe this weather? No, can you?" My mother and Luke are at the playground. My father has walked out to buy milk. I can have a moment of peace.

When I'm bored with reading, I watch some kids playing outside Charlie Parker's house. Street hockey. Soon, a man in a jean jacket joins them, grabbing a stick and firing a few balls at the goal, dodging in and out of defenders, laughing. With his blond hair and slim build, he could be a kid himself. But when the sun hits his face, I see who it is.

For a second I can't move. Then something crazy takes over, and I'm flying off the porch toward my father.

"What do you think you're doing?"

Charlie and his friends turn around. So does my dad.

"Hey, Sammy," he says.

"You're supposed to be buying milk!" I'm yelling and I can feel the tears in my eyes. "What are you? Drunk?"

The look on Charlie's face says it all. *What's wrong with you, psycho?* But I don't give him time to come up with answers. I'm already running back toward the house.

When I reach the front steps, my dad is next to me.

"Sam." His voice is soft and low. He sets a gallon of milk on the sidewalk.

All I can do is shake my head.

"Sammy." One hand on my shoulder.

"No!" I say, pulling away. "You do not get to touch me!"

My father holds his palms to the air. The what-am-I-supposed-to-do pose. "Help me out here," he says.

I look at him, furious. "Help yourself out."

But then I see his eyes, wet like mine. And I can't find any more words.

*　　*　　*

"It's different this time," he tells me as we sit on the porch swing, drinking lemonade. "I don't know why. I just know that it is."

"But *how*? *How* do you know for sure?"

"I can't explain it, Sammy. You just have to believe me."

"Well, I don't."

"Well, I give you my word. One drink a day. Tops."

I make a scoffing sound. "And the Cliché of the Century Award goes to . . ."

"That's not fair."

I stare at my father. "That's not *fair*? Me. *I* am not being fair."

"Okay. Okay." He holds up his hands like he's surrendering.

I swallow the rest of my lemonade, balance the glass on my lap. "*I'm* not being fair. That's brilliant."

"Point taken," my dad says. "Bad father, liar, not to be trusted. Nothing he can say to change your mind. A lost cause." He shifts on the swing to face me. "Well, I guess I know where I stand."

"I guess you do."

For a minute, we just sit there, silent. Then my father turns his head, looks out into the side yard. "I'm proud of you, Sammy," he says.

"*What?*"

"I'm proud of you. You're a tough cookie."

"I don't get that expression," I say. "What *is* that — tough cookie? I'm stale? It doesn't mean anything."

"Yeah, it does. You're strong. You say what you mean."

"Yeah, well. I mean what I say. And I don't believe you."

"I know you don't."

Sitting on the porch with my father, telling the truth, is weird. Part of me wants to get up and run inside. Too uncomfortable. The other part wants to crawl into his lap and stay there.

I look at my dad's arms, the golden curly hairs on them. "I want to," I say. "I want to believe you more than anything."

"I know."

My father reaches out his hand to me, and for the first time in a long time, I take it.

"This time is different," he tells me. "I can't tell you why. I just feel it."

And I can't help nodding along. For a nanosecond, I let myself believe him.

CHAPTER TEN

The eighth-grade boys have developed a rating system. They call it the Best of the Best. It is mostly body parts, but occasionally they throw in a non-looks category to give the non–Molly Katzs of this world hope. Like Best Laugh.

All week, a sheet of orange paper hangs in Danny Harmon's locker. Heavily guarded. But then, after the weekend, the list comes down and the girls are allowed to see it.

On Monday morning, the gym locker room is chaos. Everyone crowds around the mirrors, checking out hair and smoothing on lip gloss and pretending they don't know exactly what day it is.

We four are leaning against the wall by the door. Playing it cool.

"New barrette?" Tracey says to me.

"Yeah."

"Nice."

"Thanks."

I elbow Angie. "What did Marybeth do this weekend?"

"The usual."

"Snuck out?"

"Yup."

This is what Marybeth does: climbs out her bedroom

window in the middle of the night and goes to meet boys. Plus, she smokes. I know this for a fact because I have smelled Marybeth first thing in the morning. Stale and tangy like an old shoe.

"Is she grounded again?" V. asks.

"Naturally," Angie says. Then she scans the locker room. "Where's Carrot Legs?"

I look around, too. "Who knows?"

Right on cue, Molly Katz sweeps through the door. Tight red jeans and wedge heels to match. She takes her post atop the trash can. Then she raises her hand like a teacher.

"Good morning, ladies."

"Good morning, Molly!" the eighth-grade girls chorus. What they mean is, *Get out the list, princess. Pronto.* But you don't say things like that to Molly Katz. You let her do all the talking.

"Okay," Molly says, sliding a square of orange paper out of her pocket.

Angie gives a snort. "Could her jeans be any tighter?"

"Could you be any more jealous?" I say, to which Angie elbows me in the ribs.

"Ow!"

"I'm not jealous," Angie whispers. "I'm just concerned about her circulation."

"Okayyy," Molly Katz says again, taking her sweet time unfolding the paper, then reading it silently to herself. After a minute, she looks up, smiles brilliantly. "Category one. Best Smile . . . Molly Katz!"

In a semicircle around the trash can stand Molly's best

friends. Six of them, all in colored jeans and wedges, applaud wildly.

"Category two. Best Eyes . . . Ohmygosh, how embarrassing . . . Molly Katz!"

This is not a surprise. For the last three Mondays, it has been the same thing. Best Hair, Molly Katz. Best Legs, Molly Katz. Except for an occasional nod to one of Molly's underlings — Best Butt, Greta La Pia; Best Lips, Dawn West — it is a clean sweep.

"Shocker," Angie mutters.

"Seriously," I say. "Let's go."

"Wait."

"Why? This is dumb."

"Just wait."

And then, there it is. My name. Out of the shiny pink mouth of Molly Katz.

"Samantha Gwynn . . . Samantha Gwynn?"

Molly Katz is scanning the locker room. "Where are you? . . . Best Boobs? Hellooo?" Molly waits.

Everyone turns and stares at me.

"Hello," I mumble.

Molly Katz lets out a little giggle. Then her eyes get squinty. She exclaims, "They're not *kidding!*" And all of her friends start giggling, too.

I make my eyes look straight ahead, at the clock over the sink. *I will not fold my arms over my chest, I will not fold my arms over my chest, I will not fold my arms over my chest.* Instead, I concentrate on the second hand, ticking its way around the face of the clock.

When Molly Katz moves on to Category 12, Best Overall Package, Tracey rests her fingers on my arm. "Congrats," she whispers.

I stare at her. "Why?"

"Because."

"Because? You call that a reason?"

"Because," Angie says, "you just crossed over."

*　　*　　*

"Think about it," Angie tells me as we sit at the lunch table. "The only people who ever win are Molly and her friends, right?"

"So?"

"So, they're the only girls the boys ever go for. Are you with me?"

"No."

"Come *on*, Sam. You can get anyone you want now. Jeremy Thatcher? Scott Burns?"

"Tommy *Doyle*?" Tracey says.

I make a scoffing sound. "Please."

"It's true."

"Uh-huh."

"Anyone," Vanessa says, "except for Danny Harmon. He's taken."

Angie smiles. "Thanks, V."

"You're welcome."

"Right," I say. "Did anyone do the math homework yet?"

Everyone just looks at me. After a moment Angie throws up her hands like she's had it.

"Fine," I say. "Let's say I could get anyone I wanted. What makes you think I would want one of those guys? Jeremy Thatcher, for instance. What's so great about him?"

Angie shrugs. "Gorgeous, good at sports, cool. Isn't a skate rat. Doesn't have to be told to wear deodorant. Like Marybeth says, prime dating material." She looks at me almost scoldingly. "Have you not been listening to Marybeth?"

"Of course I've been listening to Marybeth."

"Okay, then," Angie says. "Jeremy Thatcher it is."

A conversation with Angie is like this. When she has made her point, the case is closed.

Except for this time.

"I don't think so, Angie," I say.

"What?"

"I'm pretty sure I like someone else."

"Shut up!"

"You like someone?" Vanessa says. "And you didn't tell us?"

I smile and shrug. I have kept Green Cap Boy Drew to myself for so long, it's like he doesn't even exist in my world outside the library.

"Who is he?" Angie says. Then, "And what's with the crap-eating grin?"

Tracey frowns. "You don't have to curse."

"*Crap* isn't a curse."

"Of course it is."

"No. It's not. Crap is a bodily function. As in, 'I ate so many burritos, I have to go take a *crap* now.'"

Tracey wrinkles her nose. "You are so foul."

"Now, a crap-eating *grin*, taken literally —"

Vanessa claps a hand over Angie's mouth. "Ignore her, Tracey. She was raised by wolves."

Angie wriggles free. "As I was saying, *crap* isn't a curse. But if you want to hear me *curse* —"

Tracey is horrified. "No!"

"How did I get to be friends with such a priss?" Angie says, shaking her head sadly.

"I'm not a *priss*. I just don't like offensive language. I find it . . ."

"Offensive?" Vanessa offers.

"Yes."

"Fine." Angie turns to me again, rolling her eyes. "Pray tell, Samantha," she says, affecting a British accent, "to what may we attribute that . . . that . . . *ludicrous* facial expression?"

To Tracey she says, "Satisfied?"

Tracey nods. "That was lovely, Angela."

I take a second to make my face as serious as possible. "What facial expression?"

"Gwynn," says Angie, "you're not planning to mess with me, are you? Because if you mess with me . . ."

"I don't know what you're talking about," I say, but as I say it, the smile creeps back onto my face.

"There!" Angie yells. "Did you see that?"

"Yup," Tracey says.

Vanessa nods. "Definitely crap-eating."

I let my face break wide open. "Oh, well," I say. "I guess I'm just going to *have* to tell you. . . ."

"You have three seconds," Angie says, holding up a cup of chocolate pudding. "Tell us or this goes on your head. One . . . two . . ."

"Okay." I hold a finger to my lips. I pause for dramatic effect. "His name is Drew. He's in high school. I met him at the library. And . . ."

"And?" Vanessa says.

"And," I say, "I don't know. I think he likes me."

Everyone is looking at me.

"Kinda."

"*Kinda?*" Angie says. "*Kinda* requires some explanation."

"Fine."

For the rest of lunch, the subject is Drew. Every tiny detail I can think of — the way he rolls the sleeves of his sweatshirt up just so, the way he chomps on his pencil when he's concentrating, the way his smile juts off to one side.

But not the way he stares at my chest. That is something my friends don't need to know.

* * *

After school, I walk home instead of taking the bus. On the way I pass Grant Park, where a man and a ponytailed girl in a baseball jersey are having a catch.

"Flick your wrist at the end," the man says. "Like this."

"Daaaad," the girl says, "I *am.*"

I stand at the fence watching them. I know I shouldn't be spying, but it's as if my head and my feet have different priorities.

"That's it, honey!" the dad yells. "Perfect!"

I watch as the dad walks over to his daughter and puts his arm around her. He leans down and whispers something in her ear that makes her laugh. And then they start walking slowly across the field toward the parking lot, still wearing their baseball gloves, bumping hips. I have an urge to follow them. But my feet won't move.

Instead I watch until they climb into their car — a red Jeep with the top down — and drive away.

CHAPTER ELEVEN

A.J.K.

Do you know a guy in your school called Drew? He mostly wears this one green baseball cap all the time. Blue, blue eyes. Just curious.

SAM

Just Sam,

Yes, I know him. Everybody knows him. Drew Maddox. Junior class rep, captain of the hockey team, etc. I'll just tell you one thing and leave it at that: <u>Be careful</u>. That's it.

There's nothing I despise more than people telling other people what to do. So I'm not telling you what to do. I'm just offering a tiny bit of advice, sage high schooler that I am.

A.J.K.

P.S. Dad situation? Update, please.

A.J.K.

Well, I am giving him one more chance.
ONE. It has been three days... and so
far so good. Of course I am watching him
like the FBI every second. Which means
not just the smell test but checking all
the bottles I know are hidden to see if
the levels go down. And making sure he is
in his bed at night when he is supposed to
be. As you can imagine, this takes up a lot
of my time, which is why I have not been
to the library in days.
    Right this second my dad is in his
office working and it is 6:30 at night. He
came home for dinner — if you can believe
it — and his words weren't even slurring.
So I have to give it to him. He is finally
putting his money where his mouth is.
Maybe it is all about the Feingold project,
which is pretty much the main topic of
every conversation. Feingold this and
Feingold that and "Mr. Feingold wants
5 billion dollars worth of panoramic
windows and cathedral ceilings by
tomorrow." I guess who cares what the
reason is. If you could see my mother,
sitting across from him, spooning out
mashed potatoes with a humongo smile,

and nodding a mile a minute, you would think she was deranged. I actually think she's just happy, but that makes me want to say, "Don't get too comfortable, Mom." But then she looks at him all Bambi eyed, and I don't want to ruin the moment. So I stay quiet.

After I leave this note for you I am going to walk by Drew's table. Drew Maddox. It has a certain ring to it. I have been saying it to myself in my head since you told me. Drew Maddox. Drew Maddox. Drew Maddox, hockey captain. Drew Maddox, class rep. Don't worry — Angie's sister Marybeth already gave me the big lecture on high school boys and how they think with a certain part of their bodies. I will not do anything stupid. Okay, "big sister"? I promise.

xo, Sam

P.S. What did you mean a few notes back, the part about if your dad ever found out the truth he wouldn't want to be related? That sounds pretty harsh to me. What did you do, anyway? Rob a bank? Kidnap a baby? Drugs? Whatever it is, you can tell me. If you want.

CHAPTER TWELVE

It's been a week since my dad's one-drink-tops pledge, and I have been checking the bottles daily. It's Sunday morning, and while I'm not completely sure, I think there's been a change. The Jim Beam bottle under the towels in the linen closet looks brand-new — with only an inch or so missing. I seem to remember that yesterday the bottle was half empty. And it wasn't Jim Beam, either — it was something else. Jack Daniel's, I think.

Or was Jack Daniel's the one in the garage?

I should have written it all down: the locations and the brands and the levels, everything. That way I would be positive.

At breakfast, it's just me and my mother. Luke is already at a playdate down the street.

"Where's Dad?" I ask.

My mom pours orange juice into my glass. "Sleeping in. He was up all night working."

"How do you know?"

"Excuse me?"

"How do you know what he was doing all night?"

My mother puts down the juice carton and looks at me. "I know because that's what he told me. And I believe him."

I nod. "Okay."

Mom sighs. She seems irritated. At *me*. Which makes me

irritated right back. Am *I* the one who's been sneaking around hiding bottles all over the house?

"*What?*" I say. "I said *okay.*"

"Saying it and meaning it are two different things, Samantha."

Which is, of course, my point exactly.

When she is busy at the sink, I take a good look at her. Washing dishes in her gray yoga pants, her hair tied back with a piece of yarn. *What's wrong with you?* I want to say. *Why don't you get it?*

I think about the baseball dad from the park. And about Vanessa's dad, Mr. Barton, who is always joking around when we sleep over, saying, "What did I do to deserve four such beautiful daughters?" Of course I am not such a goober to say it out loud, but sometimes I wish it were true. I like to imagine what my life would be like if Vanessa's dad were my dad. Nothing close to now, that's for sure.

My mom is wiping her hands on a dish towel before hanging it on a hook next to the sink. She turns to me and opens her mouth like she's about to say something, then closes it and shakes her head.

"What?" I ask her.

"Nothing."

"Mom. Come on."

She picks up the dish towel again and begins wiping the counter. "I know this isn't easy for you, Sammy," she says quietly.

I don't say anything. I just watch as my mother rubs the same spot over and over.

"But your dad is doing the best he can."

The best he can? I stare at her.

"What he really needs right now is our support. . . . He needs to know his family is behind him."

It's as if she has a bunch of note cards in front of her and she's reading out the catchphrases one by one. Like my father is running for class president and she is his campaign manager. Can she count on my vote next Thursday?

"Well," I say, "there are whiskey bottles all over the house. I check them every day, and I know for a fact he's still drinking."

"Oh, Sam."

Oh, Sam?

I can't tell what the look on my mom's face means. Is she disappointed? Angry? Sad?

I want to say, *Oh, Mom* right back at her.

She stops wiping the counter and turns around, looking me straight in the eye. "I know this is hard for you."

"Yeah. You said that."

"But —"

"But what?"

Now my mom's chin is getting quavery, and she's looking at me as if I am the adult all of a sudden. "But it's hard for me, too."

She's crying now. I have made my mother cry. And a mean, horrible part of me is glad.

"So why do you keep on believing him?" I ask.

"Because," my mom says.

Because? Isn't my mother the one who is always telling me *because* isn't a real answer?

"Because . . . I don't know what else to do."

I'm not sure why this answer makes me feel better. But somehow it does. It makes me walk across the kitchen and hand my mom a napkin, so she can blow her nose.

* * *

I've got to give my father this: He is a good actor. By dinner, he's playing the part of the family man again, asking questions about our day.

I follow the script of the good daughter, but I don't look in my father's eyes, not once. Half the time I am thinking about the whiskey bottles and how he's a pathetic hypocrite and how I want to throw lima beans at him. The other half I can't help thinking that at least he's trying.

The whole time my mom is smiling-hopeful. Luke is smiling-clueless. But I am not smiling-anything. I am just watching and trying to read my father's mind.

After dinner, he is in his office, bent over his drafting table, blueprints for the Feingold project spread out everywhere. I stand in the doorway, silent.

For a second, I have the insane notion to tell him everything. About Green Cap Boy Drew, and Charlie Parker, and A.J.K.'s notes, and the boob fruit. And I want to ask him, "Dad, what do you think?" And have him say, "Come on in, Sammy. Let's talk it through."

But then my father looks up at something on the wall, and his forehead is full of wrinkles and the bags under his eyes are the color of plums. All I can get myself to do is stand there. Then I tiptoe away.

*　*　*

I am in the stacks, trying to leave a note for A.J.K. The problem is, I'm not alone. Shelving Guy is here, doing his Eeyore routine. Shuffling, staring at the floor, taking half an hour to shelve a single book. As you can imagine, I'm riveted.

Right now he is six inches away from *The History of Modern Whaling,* and he is not exactly in a rush. I squint at the stacks, wait some more.

"Need help finding something?"

Shelving Guy is speaking to me. At least, I think he is. He's still looking at the floor, but his chin is tilted ever so slightly in my direction.

"No, thank you," I say politely.

"Are you doing a report or something?"

"Nope. Just browsing."

I try to step around him, but he turns toward me, raising his eyes as high as my belly button. "This is the marine life section, you know."

"Yes," I say, "I'm aware of that." I grab the nearest book and speed-walk out of the stacks, feeling his eyes on my back the whole way.

It's not until I get to the bathroom that I see what I've chosen: *The Sex Life of Sea Anemones.*

A moment later I am outside the bathroom . . . and so is Drew.

Drew Maddox.

He is smiling right at me, and I am frozen. I am that deer in the headlights you always hear about.

"You're not going to run away this time, are you?" he says.

"Uh-uh."

It's not a brilliant response, but it's all I can manage.

"Good."

I nod.

"Nice selection you have there."

"Huh?"

Drew points to my chest, where I happen to be clutching *The Sex Life of Sea Anemones* — quite possibly the most embarrassing book in the history of embarrassing books.

"You doing a report or something?"

"Uh-huh."

"Interesting topic."

"Science," I say. "Reproductive unit." Oh, I am such a goober. But at least I have remembered how to speak English.

Drew grins. "Cool."

And he is. So cool.

Finally I locate my smile muscles. I open my mouth to say, "cool," but there is no time. He is already kissing me. Drew Maddox is kissing me. Drew Maddox is *kissing* me.

And it feels so different from the boys at camp, with their braces banging around and their lizard tongues down my throat. This is the kiss of experience. Warm and firm and a little bit salty, too. It is a kiss that says, *I know exactly what I'm doing, so just follow my lead, girl.*

And I do.

CHAPTER THIRTEEN

At breakfast on Monday, as my dad sits at the table telling my mom the latest on the Feingold project, I look for clues.

His eyes are red. Is this from working all night, or are they bloodshot from drinking? As for his speech, some of the words he says convince me he's slurring. Then, in the next breath, he'll say something clear and smart like "concentric marble inlays" or "Greco-Roman column structure" and I will doubt myself.

It's not that I want him to be drunk, because I don't. I just want to know for sure either way. When he looks at us and smiles, I want to know his smile is for real. Not some kind of cover-up.

Before I leave for school, I make my rounds. There's a glass in the bathroom, next to my father's toothbrush, a drop of brown liquid in the bottom. When I dip my finger in and taste it, I get half an answer. The other half comes from the bottle behind the toilet, which was full yesterday. This morning, it's half empty.

My first instinct is to smash the bottle against the wall, to watch it shatter into a billion pieces. But then I hear Luke calling from outside the door.

"Sammy?"

"What?"

"I have to make pee!"

"Just a sec, buddy," I say.

Bottle back behind the toilet. Same exact spot as before. Just one of a dozen places where my father thinks we're too stupid to look.

Dear A.J.K.

Here is the part where I get to say I told you so. But it doesn't feel good to say it. It feels like the worst kind of hole in my stomach. You can probably guess what I'm about to tell you. My father is drinking again. And the truth is, I don't think he ever stopped. He just pretended harder.

It's dinnertime and my mother is at the Yogi Palace. Tonight there's a yogathon. It is an hour of Ashtanga followed by an hour of Vinyasa followed by an hour of meditation. It's not the fact that my mom is twisting herself into knots right now that I mind. What I mind is not being able to go to the library. No one told me I couldn't go, but I don't want to leave Luke alone with my father.

In the hallway, as my mother was putting on her coat, I tried to drop hints. "I don't think you should go," I said.

"Sam. It's a special class."

Oh! A special class! Well, in that case . . .

"Why don't you come with me?" Mom asked. "It'll do you good."

I shook my head. "I told you. I'm not leaving Luke."

My mother sighed, one hand on the doorknob. "Do you really want me to miss it? If you really want me to stay, I will."

"Do what you want," I said.

And that is what my mother did. Exactly what she wanted.

Now my father is making his version of dinner for me and Luke: frozen fish sticks and baked beans from a can. He is passing the tartar sauce. He is telling us he will be working on the Feingold project all night, and he would appreciate it if we would keep the noise level down.

"Okay, Daddy!" Luke yells.

I want to laugh in my dad's face. Hearing the King of Slamming and Yelling asking *us* to be quiet is downright hilarious. Forget architecture — he should consider a career in stand-up.

The irony is, my father doesn't get his own jokes. This is one of the first things I figured out. When he drinks, he doesn't remember what he did the night before. He'll come downstairs in the morning and stare at the broken plate on the floor and say, "What happened here?"

But he won't remember slamming it against the wall. He won't remember yelling at my mother because there wasn't any goddamn milk.

When I think about it, I get mad.

"Maybe you should try getting yourself some earplugs," I say.

My dad looks up from his fish sticks. "Maybe you could try cutting me a little slack, hey, pal?"

Once again I am astounded. If anyone should be cutting anyone slack around here, it should be *him*.

"Come on," I say to Luke. "Let's go upstairs."

Our father nods. "Great idea."

"Thanks!" Luke says.

"You won't even know we're in the house," I say. "It'll be like we're dead."

*   *   *

Later, Luke is bored with upstairs. Also, he is thirsty. And no, he does not want water from the bathroom sink. He wants grape juice and cranberry juice mixed. Just like Mommy makes it.

Well, what is a person supposed to do? Let him wither away from dehydration?

I bring Luke downstairs to the living room. I go into the kitchen to pour juice. When I get back, the Wiggles are blasting and Luke is in full bounce-and-flop mode, singing his little heart out.

"Wiggle with me, Sammy!"

I look at the door to my father's study. I think about him sitting at the desk, pulling the bottle out of the second drawer on the left, taking a long swig. Then another. Then another.

I look at Luke, shaking his hips and giggling. Free as can be.

I hop up on the couch next to Luke and just let loose. I

bounce and flop and sing, but the whole time I am watching the door to the study, waiting.

One one-thousand . . . two one-thousand . . . three one-thousand —

"Hey!"

There it is.

"Keep it down out there!"

At the sound of his voice, the usual pit forms in my stomach. But along with it, a white-hot flash of anger in my chest.

"*What?*" I yell, mid-bounce. "We can't hear you!"

Luke laughs, then yells, "We can't hear you!"

"We can't hear you!" we yell together.

That's when the door to the study swings open and he stumbles out, a fistful of blueprints in one hand. In the other, a near-empty bottle of Jim Beam.

I feel the pit in my stomach grow. But the white-hot flash in my chest is bigger than the pit in my stomach. I jump off the couch and stand facing my father.

I want to place a single finger on his breastbone and push. I want to raise my lip into a sneer and say, *Look at yourself. You think you're an architect, but really you're just a bum.*

The only thing that stops me is Luke, who is still bouncing away on the couch, thinking it's all a game.

"Wiggle with me, Daddy!" Luke jumps next to our father and throws his hands into the air. He forgets he's holding a full cup of juice.

What happens next is like a slow-motion movie clicking by, frame by single frame:

Juice flying through the air.

Click, click, click.

Juice splashing against the Feingold project blueprints.

Click, click, click.

Dad raising the bottle in the air above Luke's head.

Click, click, click.

Bottle cracking against Luke's face.

Click, click, click.

Blood. Everywhere.

CHAPTER FOURTEEN

On the way to the hospital, I forget whose car we're in. I'm too busy pressing towels to Luke's face and whispering that everything will be okay.

But then I look up, and I see Charlie Parker's mom. I see the back of her shag hairdo in the driver's seat. And I remember that only minutes ago I was standing on the Parkers' front lawn, holding Luke and screaming like a lunatic. *Help! Hellllp!*

I have only one question: Why didn't I just ring the doorbell?

Right now Luke is strapped into Faye's booster seat, looking smaller than small. He is not crying so much as whimpering. Underneath the towels, his face is a big red mess that I am trying not to think about.

I swallow, blink.

I think about how the next time Luke wants one more story before bed, I will read it to him. Even if he wants the dump truck book. I will read and read, until he falls asleep.

*   *   *

My mother arrives just after Luke is wheeled down the hall. She is still wearing her yoga turban. In the fluorescent lights, against the backdrop of puke-green walls, she looks old.

The first thing she does is hug me.

"I'm sorry," she says. "I'm so sorry."

Over and over again, she says it. *I'm so sorry, Sammy.* The whole time, rocking me back and forth like a baby.

At first, I keep my arms to my sides, stiff as a board. But before long, I am crying. I'm crying so hard my mom can't hold me up anymore, and we have to sit.

*   *   *

My mother, Charlie's mother, and a doctor with silver hair are standing across the waiting room by the coffee machine, talking in hushed tones. I try to hear what they're saying, but I can't make it out.

At one point Mrs. Parker puts her arm around my mom's shoulders and squeezes. They both dab their eyes with tissues from Mrs. Parker's purse.

I try to distract myself, but the magazines on the table are the boring kind. A pile of *Reader's Digest*s and yesterday's newspaper with crumbs all over it. I have already had two orange sodas and a bag of pretzels from the vending machine. I contemplate buying a Snickers, but then I find all I have left in my pocket is a dime.

Charlie Parker sits two chairs away, not because he wants to, but because his dad made him. "Charlie's here to support you," Mr. Parker said when he dropped him off.

Yeah right.

Charlie is staring at the TV, which is tuned to Lifetime: Television for Women — our most unfavorite channel. Once when we were both home sick with the chicken pox, we were allowed to watch TV all day in the Parkers' basement. By day three, we got so bored we watched a Lifetime original movie marathon. Sometimes the acting was so bad we would laugh until we had coughing fits, until even our chicken pox hurt.

Now I can't imagine laughing.

"Lifetime," Charlie says in his best falsetto. "Television for Nutjobs." He stands, hikes up his supersize jeans. "Come on. Let's go find out about your brother."

*　　*　　*

Mrs. Parker arranges four hard orange chairs into a square. She says we should all sit down so we can talk.

"Mom?" I can hear the panic rising in my own voice. "Is Luke okay?"

But Mrs. Parker is the one who answers. "Your brother's going to be fine, honey. He has a fracture —" She pauses to draw an imaginary line across the right side of her face. "Here. On his cheekbone. And he's had some stitches."

"How many?" I say.

"Twenty-four."

I sit there, nodding, trying to imagine it. Twenty-four stitches. That sounds like Luke's whole face.

Then Charlie opens his big fat cake hole. "Is he gonna have a scar?" Like the prospect is thrilling to him.

"Charles!" Mrs. Parker says sharply.

"What?" Charlie looks at his mom. Then he looks down and mutters, "Sorry."

Well. Now I am sickly curious. "Is he?" I ask.

"Luke is going to be just fine," Mrs. Parker says. "He's a very lucky little boy."

By this stage, I know there is a lie brewing, and I am not about to back down.

"Is he going to have a scar?"

I stare at my mother, who is staring at her hands. "Mom . . . *Mom.*"

Finally she looks up. "Maybe." She takes in a breath, lets it out. "Probably. Yes."

I nod.

"He may need some . . . cosmetic surgery."

"Oh." The word sticks in my throat like a glob of peanut butter. *Oh.*

Suddenly I don't want to look at anyone. I don't want them to see what I know is true: *I let this happen. I let Luke come downstairs, and I let him be loud, and I let him —*

"Sam?"

It's Mrs. Parker talking, with her hand on my arm. She has always had nice hands, soft and creamy, with just a touch of pink polish on the nails. I've never met anyone else who takes such good care of her hands. My mother's never even had a manicure. But Mrs. Parker wears special gloves, even to sleep in. When I was younger and staying over at their house, if I woke up scared she would rub my back with the gloves on.

"Sam?" she says again, gently.

I can feel everyone's eyes on me. To my left, Charlie's foot is tapping the floor. *Taptaptaptaptaptaptap.* It's his nervous knee jiggle that I know so well, that always bugs me so much.

Taptaptaptaptaptaptaptaptaptap. Besides that, the room is silent.

"Honey," Mrs. Parker says, "we need to talk about your dad."

I nod, because I know that if I try to open my mouth I will start crying again. And I don't want to cry anymore.

"Your dad," Mrs. Parker says. "Well. He needs help, Sammy."

"I know," I whisper.

I look up and find my mom's eyes. She is crying a little, which makes me cry a little, even though I try not to.

Then, I don't know why, but I am laughing. I am *laughing.* I am doing the opposite of what I should be doing, like shouting in the library or swearing in church. I am laughing at the most serious moment in my life.

I guess it is what you could call relief.

CHAPTER FIFTEEN

My father has been gone for three days — his usual amount. Only this time it's different. This time we actually know where to find him.

Shady Brook Farm, the place is called, which sounds nice. But when I ask my mother about the farm and the brook and the shade, I learn that there are no animals, no freshwater sources, and no trees to speak of, so whoever came up with the name must have either been a nutcase or had a sick sense of humor.

I didn't exactly get to say good-bye. It was more of a wave from the Parkers' front porch as my mom drove by and honked. She wanted to drop him off alone, which was okay by me. Personally, I think she should have let him hitchhike and take his chances. Maybe the deranged psycho with the metal hook for an arm — the one they warn you about at camp — would pick him up. That is what my English teacher, Mr. Schmidt, would call poetic justice.

Luke is home from the hospital and looking like a small relative of Frankenstein. The first time I saw him I almost fell over. Now I am getting used to it. I find if I focus on the left side of his face I'm okay. It is the right side that shocks you — all purple and puffy, with a jagged line of black sutures running from the edge of his nose to his ear. Then there's his eye, where the white part isn't white anymore, it's red. The doctor said it's just broken blood vessels that will go back to normal in a week or so.

Normal.

It's only been three days, but already life is the opposite of normal. For one thing, my mother has stopped answering the phone. Nana keeps leaving messages, but no one calls her back. Then, there are the Parkers who have taken over. Charlie's mom has been cooking nonstop and his dad has decided to rake up all our leaves and stuff them into big brown bags. It is obvious he is trying to be the R.D. — Replacement Dad — but here is the joke: I've never seen my own father pick up a rake in his life. He always paid some high school kid to do his dirty work.

Tonight, all four Parkers show up with lasagna and board games. My mother answers the door, fake smiling, saying how nice it is for them to stop by. But I can see what she is really thinking: *Enough already, you people.*

After dinner, we play Monopoly. Charlie sits across the table from me, shaking his head and muttering curse words the whole time.

"Charles!" Mrs. Parker says, every time he lets one fly.

"What?" Charlie says back. "I said son of a *witch.*"

When he lands on Boardwalk, which I own with three hotels, he gets up off his chair and starts yelling at the ceiling, "Why, for the love of Zeus? Why?"

I know he is doing this for my benefit, to try to make me laugh. But I don't laugh. I just hold out my hand for the rent money.

Later, we're sitting on the steps outside. Charlie's nervous knee is bouncing away.

"Knock it off," I say.

"What?"

I put my hand on his leg. "That."

"Oh."

We don't say anything for a minute, and I can tell it is killing him to keep that leg still. But he is trying.

"So," Charlie says finally, "how's your brother doing?"

I can feel my chest get tight when he asks this. "*You* saw him," I say.

"No, I mean . . . how's he, you know, *do*ing?"

"Oh . . ." I look out into the yard, so Charlie can't see my lying face. "Fine. Good."

"Good."

I nod. "Uh-huh."

I leave out the small detail that Luke has been waking up in the middle of the night for the last three nights, crying.

"Too bad he missed Halloween," Charlie says.

"What?"

"Halloween. He wouldn't have needed a costume."

He's smiling. As if he said the funniest thing ever.

I stand up, silent for a moment. I contemplate grabbing the potted plant on the railing and bashing Charlie Parker's head in. But I realize there has been enough head-bashing for one week. So instead, I make my voice ice cold. "I can't believe I used to be friends with you."

Charlie looks up. "Sam. Come on." His face is twisted with something. Shame? Regret? Good!

"Come on, *what*?"

"I didn't mean it that way. I was just trying to make a —"

"Joke?" I say. "You were just trying to make a *joke*? What, you think this is *funny*? You think this is something to *laugh* about? My father bashes my little brother's face in with a bottle, and you think it's *funny*?"

"No!" Charlie is standing now, too. "I don't think it's funny! I don't . . . I didn't know what else to say! Okay? I'm just trying to be your friend!"

"Well, you can stop trying. Because you're not."

Charlie stands in front of me, staring, and I am staring right back. It is a stare-down. A stare-off. Whoever looks away first loses.

I will not look away. I will not look away. I will not look away. I will not look away. I will not look away.

Charlie looks away.

Ha!

When he looks back again, his face is different. Quiet-serious. "I didn't do it, by the way."

"What."

"I didn't take your bra that time. I know you think it was me, but it wasn't."

I don't say anything.

Charlie starts to leave, then stops. "I just thought you should know," he says. "Even if you don't believe me."

"I don't."

"Well, it's the truth."

"Well, tell it to the judge."

Charlie shakes his head. "Thanks a lot, Sam."

"Yeah," I say, "thanks to you, too, *Chuck*. Thanks for nothing."

Charlie goes to leave again. I wait for him to whip around with some snappy comeback, some Charlie Parker classic.

But this time he doesn't look back. He keeps right on walking down the steps, onto the sidewalk. Away from me.

Well. I got in the last word. I won.

Then why do I feel so empty?

CHAPTER SIXTEEN

On Monday, the girls are waiting by my locker. They scream when they see me. *Sammmmmmmy!* Then there's the hugging.

They don't have a clue.

"How *are* you?" Tracey says.

"Fine," I say.

"You look good," Vanessa says.

"Yeah? You should have seen me on Friday." I make myself laugh, a little *heh, heh, heh.* "I was one big pus-ball."

Tracey wrinkles her nose. "Gross."

Well, she's right. Pinkeye *is* gross. I got it once in third grade. The whole class did. Conjunctivitis, the school nurse called it. We had to put drops in our eyes every morning, ointment at night.

"Don't worry," I say. "I'm not contagious anymore."

Everyone nods.

Why shouldn't they believe me? I've never lied to them before. Not technically.

I open my locker, take out my English binder. "How's the Danny Harmon situation?" I ask Angie, changing the subject. "Any developments?"

Angie just looks at me, shakes her head. That's when I

realize she hasn't spoken a word since I got here. Tracey and V. have been doing all the talking.

I pretend to be busy in my locker, looking for a pen, but really I'm thinking. About the series of phone calls my mother made over the weekend, "private" ones, from my dad's office, which she doesn't know has a vent in the ceiling that happens to connect to the floor of my room.

Patrick has had a medical emergency, she told my father's boss. *He's going to need some time off.*

At least a month, is what she said. *Six weeks at the most. . . . No, no, nothing like that. His doctors anticipate a full recovery. . . . Yes, of course he understands that the Feingold project will have to continue without him.*

Next was Luke's preschool teacher, who my mom wanted to give a "heads-up" about the "accident" Luke had on Thursday night. Nothing serious. Just a few stitches.

I stopped listening after that; I'd heard enough. But now it occurs to me that there may have been other calls. Like to Angie's parents.

Or maybe I am just going crazy.

"Angie," I say, "what was the math homework?"

Angie rolls her eyes. "Review problems. Stupid chapter seven quiz tomorrow."

"Cool," I say.

"*Excuse* me?"

I take out my assignment book and write *Algebra Quiz*, a casual scrawl. "Don't worry. We'll study seventh period, 'kay?"

"Whatever. I'll bomb it, anyway."

"Hey." I punch Angie lightly on the shoulder. "Nice attitude."

The bell rings. Bodies start moving. I can breathe again.

*   *   *

After lunch, I am in French class, not listening, writing to A.J.K. I am telling her everything about everything. About how the first thing I did after my father hit Luke was to yell at him like he was the kid and I was the parent. How I pointed to the red leather chair by the fireplace and said, in a voice that wasn't mine, "Sit there. Sit there and think about what you've done." And how my father actually did it. He sat on the edge of the chair and stared at the piece of broken bottle in his hand. Just stared at it, like he had no idea how it got there. And when we got home from the hospital, hours later, he was still in that spot, passed out. The broken bottle in his hand.

"Mademoiselle Samantha?"

It is the French teacher, Madame Gettier.

"*Ma-de-moi-selle Sa-man-tha,*" she says again, through cupped hands.

I look up from my notebook. "*Oui?*"

Madame makes clucking sounds. She does this with a French accent, which you may not think is possible, but is. The French cluck of disapproval.

"*Je suis désolé,*" I say. *I am sorry.* Which is one of the first things I learned how to say this year. That, and "*S'il vous plaît peux je plaire vais aux toilettes?*" *Please may I go to the toilet?* Which is what I say now.

Madame knots her eyebrows at me. *"Non!"* she says. *"Absolutement pas!"* She taps my French book with her pointer. *"Fais attention, Simone!"*

"Oui," I say.

And go right back to A.J.K.

*　*　*

After school I go to the library and get stuck talking to Miss Howe, which wouldn't have happened if the yearbooks were in a logical place. The reference section, for instance. Now that would make sense. But no. They are kept in a big glass case behind the checkout desk, padlocked, like they are billion-year-old Egyptian scrolls.

I stand in front of Miss Howe for a good long while, watching her stamp books with a little red stamper. *Page flip. Stamp. Stack. Page flip. Stamp. Stack. Page flip. Stamp. Stack.* Then I get tired of waiting and start to walk away. This is when Miss Howe decides to notice me.

"May I help you?"

Well, *yes*, Enid, as a matter of fact you may.

I walk back over. "Could I see a high school yearbook, please? This year's?"

"The annual," she says in her pinchy voice, "isn't issued until the spring."

I nod. "Okay. Last year's, then."

Miss Howe looks at me over the tops of her glasses. She purses her lips and I regret not leaving when I had the chance.

Once in seventh grade, I tried to check out a book from the

young adult section — **<u>For mature readers ONLY</u>** — and she acted the same way. She looked at me all pursy-lipped and asked how old I was. *"Twelve,"* I said. *"A very mature twelve."* And she snatched the book right out of my hand. Like I was a criminal.

"Annuals may not be checked out," she says now.

"I don't need to check it out."

"And they may *not* be written in."

I nod. "Right."

Miss Howe looks at me for another few seconds, then turns to unlock the glass case. When she hands me the yearbook she says, "Stay in this room. Where I can keep an eye on you."

She is leaning in so close I can see the little hairs on her upper lip. A whole army of them, bleached blond. I can smell the egg salad on her breath.

"Yes," I say. And go to sit in the corner.

*　　*　　*

Here is what I get from the *James Madison High School Goldbug*: not much. In the freshman class there are no A.J.K.'s whatsoever. In the sophomores there is one, but the J. isn't for Jessup, it's for Jean. *Andrea Jean King.* Andrea Jean King has frizzy hair, thick glasses, and zits. She doesn't exactly look like the type to make the soccer team, let alone belt out a show tune duet with Tom Lombardo. Juniors: one Alexandra J. Klein and one Amanda J. Kunkel, but I have never seen them in the library. And the seniors have already graduated.

Well. I am beginning to think A.J.K. is a fraud. Or a figment of my imagination. Or Charlie Parker, messing with my mind. Or . . . wait a second. Maybe the letters are not initials at all. Maybe they are a little code I am supposed to crack.

Always **J**udge **K**angaroos

Apricot **J**uice **K**ool-Aid

After **J**umping, **K**iss

Yuh. I don't think so.

The one good part of the yearbook is Drew. Drew Maddox, page 74. His class photo is movie-star handsome, all floppy hair and white teeth. It makes you want to lean in and kiss his shiny face. Which I might actually do, if I were alone instead of hunched over a study carrel with Miss Howe hovering behind me, breathing egg salad on my neck.

"Are your hands clean?" she asks me.

"Pardon?"

"Your hands. Did you wash them before handling the annual?"

I stop for a moment and look at her. "My hands are clean."

Miss Howe is looking at me like she doesn't quite believe me. Like she thinks I may have deliberately made a big batch of Rice Krispies treats before picking up the yearbook.

Oh, Enid, I want to say. *Come now.*

I wait for her to tell me something else, like to only touch the corners of the pages, or not to exhale. But Miss Howe surprises me.

"Would you like to see something?" she asks.

I shrug. "Okay."

And that's when she whips it out. The *James Madison High*

School Goldbug, 1954. She puts it down in front of me and softly taps a photo with her finger. "Here."

I lean in, squint at the girl with the flipped-out hairdo and short-short bangs. She is wearing a little round-collared shirt. No, not a shirt — a *blouse.* Lipstick. Circle pin. Pearls.

Underneath the photo, three words: *Elizabeth "Libby" Howe.*

I look up at Miss Howe. "This is you?"

She nods, smiles slightly. I can see the gap between her two front teeth. Not Enid's teeth anymore. *Libby*'s teeth.

"That was the fashion in those days," she tells me. "The sawed-off haircut. Ghastly, isn't it?"

This time I smile. "It's not so bad."

Miss Howe looks at the picture and shakes her head. "A million years ago," she says. "A lifetime ago."

"Huh," I say.

"It will be you someday. Looking back. Wondering where it all went."

"Yes," I say. But I can't imagine it. Being old like Miss Howe and edgy about everything, with a mustache to bleach. I can't even picture being in high school yet.

* * *

When I get home, Luke is asleep on the couch. I cover him with a blanket, and for a moment or two I just watch him, the rise and fall of his chest. I'd like to know what his face is going to look like when the swelling goes away, and the bruises. I wonder if he will ever look like Luke again, or if he will always be different. I wonder if he will ever forget what happened here on this same couch.

Wondering this makes me mad all over again. I don't think I have ever hated my father as much as I do right now.

*   *   *

Upstairs, I lie down next to my mom. I am on *his* side of the bed, which makes me want to scratch myself all over.

"I wish we could just leave him there," I say. "On the farm with no animals."

My mother makes a little sound, like a laugh.

"I'm serious."

"I know you are," she says.

We lie there for a moment in silence.

"Your father needs us," she says quietly. "Now more than ever."

Well, I don't know what to say to that. What do you say to your mother, the broken record, that could possibly make her see the tiniest sliver of light?

So I don't say anything. I just get off the bed and go downstairs. And check on Luke.

CHAPTER SEVENTEEN

Third period, dirt science. Jacob Mann has a big brown stain on his shirt. Also, a new blond joke.

"What did the blond say when she opened the box of Cheerios?"

"I don't know," I say. "And I don't care."

"Look! Doughnut seeds!"

"Uh-huh." I open my science binder. "That's hysterical. Really. I'm convulsing with laughter."

"I know, right?" Jacob snickers. "You blonds are — wait a second. You don't *get* it, do you?"

I give him a look.

Jacob shakes his head. Grins. "You don't get it."

I take out a piece of lined paper. "Yes, I do."

"No. No, you don't."

"Shut up."

"*Ohhhhhhh.*" Jacob pretends to break down crying, uncontrollably, in front of the whole class. "Mr. Ryderrrrr," he blubbers, "Sam hurt my feeeeeeelings."

Mr. Ryder looks over at us and frowns.

"I don't know what happened," I tell him. "He's very sensitive. You know? Delicate, like a flower."

Mr. Ryder picks up a piece of chalk and writes our names on the board. "Consider yourselves warned," he says. "One more disruption and you're both staying after school."

*   *   *

By the time I get to lunch I have detention. Not from dirt science, though. From gym class. I think it was a combination of my footwear (clogs), my lack of effort (half a chin-up), and the permanent pole up Ms. Fish's rear end.

The funny thing is, I don't care. This is what I've been doing for the past week: not caring.

"Ms. Fish is such a wench," I say, unwrapping my turkey-on-rye. "You guys are so lucky you don't have her."

"I heard she yelled at you in front of everyone," Tracey says.

"Who said that?"

"Molly Katz."

"Typical."

Angie spears a Tater Tot with her fork. "Molly Katz should have her mouth wired shut. For the good of the school. For the good of the *universe*."

"Awww," I say. "That's sweet."

"Come on, Angie," Vanessa says. "She's not that bad."

Angie pierces another Tater Tot. "Yes, she is."

Angie puts down her fork. "Molly Katz." She picks up the fork again and begins attacking the entire plate of Tater Tots. "And Danny Harmon." *Stab.* "Deserve." *Stab.* "Each other." *Stab.*

"Uh," I say, "did I miss something?"

Vanessa looks at me. "Last period. In front of the boys' locker room. Remember that love scene from *Hearts Interrupted*? Instead of Ridge and Rebecca, picture Danny and Molly Katz."

I look at Tracey, who nods. "It was gross."

Angie takes one last stab at her plate before she pushes it away.

"They deserve each other," she says again, meekly.

"Angie," I say, "he's not worth it."

Tracey puts a hand on Angie's arm. "He is *so* not worth it."

"The boy has *terrible* taste," Vanessa says firmly.

Angie nods. "I know." Then she gets that look — that scrunched-up bulldog face that means she's about to start bawling any second. Sometimes, when she's just on the cusp, you can stop her by saying something funny.

"What did the blond say when she looked in the box of Cheerios?"

Angie stares at me. Then she starts bawling. "I don't knowwwww."

I lean over and hug her. "Look! Doughnut seeds!"

Angie blubbers for a few more seconds. Then she pulls away and wipes her nose with the back of her hand. "That's the stupidest thing I ever heard."

I smile. "I know."

*   *   *

After school, I am in the kitchen making muffins when the phone rings. It's Nana, and she wants to talk to my dad. She's been trying to reach him all week, she tells me. But all she gets is voice mail.

"Um," I say, spooning batter into little fluted cups, "my mom didn't call you yet?"

"No," Nana says. "Your mother did not call me."

"Interesting."

I look at my mom, who is sitting at the kitchen table playing checkers with Luke. She shakes her head at me, mouths, *I'm not here.*

"Samantha." Nana sounds annoyed.

"Guess what I'm doing right now?" I say. "Making muffins!"

"Put your mother on the phone."

"Cranberry walnut. With cream cheese frosting. From that book you gave me!"

"*Samantha.*"

"Yeah?"

"Put your mother on."

"Okay."

I hold out the phone to my mother, who frowns at me. "What do you want me to do?" I whisper. "*Lie?*"

She stands up and grabs the phone out of my hand. "Jean!" she says, her voice a few octaves higher than normal. "How *are* you?" Then she hightails it to my dad's office, where she can talk in "private."

"Hey, Lukey," I say, "let's go upstairs and play, okay?"

Luke nods. It is what he does now. The nod is the new *Great!*

*   *   *

I have to give my mother credit. She actually tells the truth this time.

"Listen, Jean," she says to Nana. "I made the only decision possible. Patrick needs help, and that is what he's getting. . . . Well, it happens to be the only rehabilitation facility we could afford."

"I'm sorry you feel that way," my mother says. "But that's the way it is."

"No, Jean. I do not care what the neighbors think."

She sounds so tough and cool and above it all. Like she believes every word she's saying.

But afterward, when I tiptoe downstairs to check on her, she is running through the house like a wild woman, opening all the windows. Even though it's freezing outside, the coldest day this fall, and we haven't turned on the heat yet.

I want to do what she would do for me, if I were the one flipping out: go over and touch her arm, tell her to take some warming breaths.

But instead I just stand and stare.

While she hyperventilates.

A. J. K.

Actually, Jellybeans Kill? Active Jugglers Kick?
  WHO ARE YOU???
  Today, my mother really let her freak flag fly. I think she's losing it. I think we all are. And it's all thanks to one special person, my father the drunk. My father the bum. My father the

Wait a second. I'm going to get my thesaurus.

Swiller.

Sot.

Toper.

Guzzler.

Tosspot.

Lush.

I like that one. Lush. My father the lush.

CHAPTER EIGHTEEN

I have mashed with Drew Maddox three times now. We can't do it every night, because his hockey practice is starting. Plus sometimes I just chicken out. I know that if I go to the library right after school he won't be there, and I can relax. I can concentrate on A.J.K. without worrying, *Is my hair okay? Does my breath smell like baked ziti?*

Tonight, here we both are. By the water fountain — our special spot.

"Hey there," Drew says, grabbing me from behind. His breath is warm on my neck.

"Hey," I say.

"I was hoping I'd see you tonight," he says.

"Oh, yeah?" I say, cool as can be on the outside, while inside my heart does a little hip-hop routine.

I let Drew turn me around so we are face-to-face. Lips to lips.

It's a funny thing, when you think about it. Kissing. Why lips? Why not elbows? Or ears? And who came up with it, anyway? I guess it would have to be the cavepeople. But they probably didn't call it *kissing* back then. They probably had their own special cave word for it, like *ooga-booga*.

Hey, honey, what say we ooga-booga?

Well, now I'm giggling. Right here in the middle of my Drewkiss.

And Drew is pulling away. "What's so funny?"

He sounds bugged. Like he thinks I'm laughing at him.

"Nothing," I say. "Your tongue tickles."

This seems to do the trick. Now he is smiling down at me, like I am the cutest thing ever.

"Hey," he says now, "what are you doing Saturday night?"

"I don't know," I say, a little tease in my voice. "What am I doing Saturday night?"

"Going to a party. With me."

"Going to a party. With you."

"Cool," he says.

I smile.

And then we mash some more.

* * *

I don't know why I lie to the girls, but I do. I've been on a roll lately.

"I can't sleep over Saturday," I tell Vanessa at lunch.

"Why not?" she asks.

"My mom needs me to babysit Luke. She's got some yoga thing."

"What?" Angie sounds annoyed. "She can't find anyone else?"

I shrug. "It's hard to get babysitters on a Saturday night."

Tracey says, "Bummer."

"I know. I don't even get *paid*. I have to do it out of the goodness of my heart."

"That stinks," Angie says.

I roll my eyes. "Tell me about it."

Liar, liar, pants on fire.

A.J.K.

Guess what????!!!!! Drew Maddox invited me to a party on Saturday and I'm going!!!!!! It is at some girl's house I've never heard of. Bethany Shaver. Do you know her? I guess she is a junior because I looked her up in the yearbook. There is this kid Andy Shaver who is in my class. I wonder if they are related? But anyway, who cares if they are. I'm going!!!!!! I've already figured out my cover story, which is simple because I always sleep over at my friend Vanessa's on Saturday nights.

I guess the only thing I need from you is WHAT TO WEAR. I am not about to show up to a high school party looking like Bridget Jones in the bunny suit, if you know what I mean.

So, help!

Love, SAM

*P.S. How relieved are you that the soc-
cer season is over???!!! Does this mean
your dad is finally off your case?*

Friday night, Luke wakes up crying. This is the eighth
night in a row — eight days since he came home from the hospital. I go to his room and climb under the covers. I wipe his
face with my pajama top, even though that means snot and
tears all over me.

We talk about happy things. Dump trucks. Golden retriev-
ers. Nana's house by the ocean and how the next time we go
there we will look for sea glass to add to our collection.

The whole time I am thinking, *Where is my mother? Isn't
this* her *job?* But I already know the answer, and that is the little bottle of sleeping pills on her bedside table — a present
from Charlie Parker's mom.

"Don't take more than one at a time," Mrs. Parker said.
"And only when you really, really can't sleep. Those things will
knock you right out."

"Of course," my mother said.

Well, according to my calculations, she has *really, really* not
been able to sleep for about eight nights now.

"Sammy?"

Luke is looking up at me.

"Yeah, buddy?"

"When is Daddy coming home?"

This makes me want to cry. Because it's the first time he's
mentioned our dad, and the question is not *Why did he bash my
face in?* but *When is he coming home?*

"I don't know." I hold my breath a little. "Do you want him to come home?"

I am hoping Luke will say, *No! What are you, crazy, Sammy? The man hit me with a bottle! He should be locked up for life!*

But this is not what my brother says. In fact, he doesn't say anything at all. He just nods.

And I think, *Brain damage.*

"Lukey," I say, "how many fingers am I holding up?"

"Three."

Fine. Not brain damage, then. Amnesia.

"What day is it tomorrow?"

"Um," Luke says, "Saturday?"

"You're right," I say. And hug him.

Tomorrow is Saturday.

CHAPTER NINETEEN

In the morning, the Parkers show up on our front porch. Charlie's mom comes bearing some stinky egg dish. "Frittata," she calls it. "Full of protein." Faye has brought her entire fleet of Barbies and styling products. Mr. Parker comes equipped with tool belt — ready to winterize anything that needs winterizing. And what does Charlie bring? Nada. Zilch. Zero. The Big Goose Egg. He probably thinks his presence is a present.

"Come on in," my mother says. She is still wearing her pajamas, which tells me she didn't know they were coming. Or she forgot.

"Lukey!" Faye and the Barbies attack my brother. "Let's go play!"

Luke nods and lets Faye lead him by the hand to his own living room.

"He looks great, Ellie," Charlie's mom says. "Just great."

The mothers make their way to the kitchen, where the sad truth is revealed: The only breakfast food we have is a moldy English muffin.

"Charlie!" Mrs. Parker calls. "Sam! I need you two to run to the store!"

*   *   *

It is the coldest grocery run in history, and I don't mean the temperature. I mean Charlie refuses to utter a single word. The entire time.

"What does your mom want us to get?" I ask.

Charlie hands me the list.

"Okay," I say, when we reach the refrigerated section. "What kind of orange juice do you want?"

Charlie shrugs, points to the Tropicana.

Then there are the bagels, which Charlie knows I have a strong opinion on. But what does he do? Picks the worst possible kind — onion and garlic — without so much as a consultation.

On and on it goes, until we arrive at my front porch again. By which point I have just about had it.

"What's your problem?" I say.

Charlie doesn't speak, but his eyebrows do. Coolly arched, they reply, *I don't have a problem. You have a problem.*

I stare right back at him. "Oh, *I* have a problem? I see."

We walk into the house.

"Yes. That makes perfect sense, Chuckles. You: problem-free. Me: difficult."

Through the hall to the dining room.

"This is *my* game, you know. The silent treatment. I *invented* this game."

Charlie makes a scoffing noise under his breath.

"See? You're not even good at it! You just scoffed. You can't *scoff* during the silent treatment."

I go right on talking. It's nauseating, and yet I cannot stop myself. I keep spewing until we get to the kitchen, where our mothers are waiting to fill our mouths.

*   *   *

It's 8:32 P.M. and I still don't have an outfit. As for A.J.K.'s "fashion tips," they are about as much help as a stick.

Sam (Sweatpants, Argyles, Moccasins),

Wear what makes you feel comfortable. Just be yourself. That goes for life, as well as for high school parties.

Anyway Just Kidding...

About the sweats — save them for the gym. Only wear argyles if you're going retro. And moccasins: <u>always</u> a mistake.

I try on everything in my closet, piece by piece. I haven't worn half of this stuff since sixth grade, but I figure these are desperate times.

Finally I settle on the jeans my mother bought me that I vowed I would never wear because they make my butt look like an apple. And a black turtleneck that actually fits, unlike the XXLs I usually wear.

Hair: Nix the ponytail. Down and loose.

Jewelry: silver horseshoe pendant from Angie.

Makeup: Where is Nana when I need her? Remember what she told me when she gave me the Makeup for Morons kit:

Less is more. Just the teeniest smidgen of mascara. Blush. Lip gloss. Done.

When I look in the mirror a part of me can't believe it. *Who are you?* I ask. The girl just smiles and flips her hair over one shoulder. She has that I'm-cool-and-hot-at-the-same-time confidence thing going on. I picture all heads turning as she walks into Bethany Shaver's house.

Who's that girl? people will whisper. *Where did she come from?*

Oh, her? Drew Maddox will say, proud as can be. *That's my girlfriend. Sam.*

*   *   *

Well, where am I supposed to park my bike?

I am standing two houses away from the party because I am suddenly, painfully aware that I am wearing a reflector jacket and a helmet.

And everyone else arrived in cars.

*   *   *

9:55 P.M.

I have finally worked up enough nerve to walk up the Shavers' front steps. My legs are so jelly-filled it's a wonder I can move at all.

"Hey," some guy on the porch swing calls to me. "How ya doin'?"

I give him a chin jerk. "Great. You?"

"Great."

I notice there's a girl sitting next to him, a redhead. It's Juliet from the library, smoking a cigarette. Wait. She *smokes*?

"It's pretty crazy in there," Juliet informs me.

"Cool," I say.

When really, I am the opposite of cool. I am sweating bombs.

Inside, the stereo is so loud you don't just hear the music, you taste it. People are everywhere — on couches, on tables, sliding down the banister.

Some guy in a hockey helmet hands me a red plastic cup. "You need to catch up!" he yells. "Keg's in the bathroom!"

I want to yell back, *Then where do I pee?!* But Hockey Helmet has already moved onto the dance floor.

For a while, I stand against the wall in the dark, pretending to drink out of my empty cup. Soon I am hip-checked out of the way by some mashing couple. No one says, "Excuse me." It's like I'm invisible without wearing the invisibility cloak.

Finally I make my way through the mass of sweaty bodies to the kitchen, where the light is. Also, where Drew is.

I spot him right away, perched on the counter. He's wearing the green baseball cap, but backwards, and a black T-shirt that fits just right. He's so cute, I want to run over and tickle him.

Be cool, I tell myself. *Let him notice you first.*

After about a million years, he does. He looks over and smiles, while I pretend to be squinting at the clock above his head. *10:35. Hmmm. Already?*

Now he is by my side. His shoulder is against my shoulder.

"Hey," he says.

"Hey," I say.

"You look great."

"Yeah?"

"Yeah."

Drew leans in, and his lips graze my earlobe. "Hey," he says again, low. His breath smells vinegary. "I'm glad you came."

I lean in, whisper back, "Me, too."

We move across the kitchen as a unit. DrewandSam. SamandDrew. His hand is on the small of my back, steering.

Suddenly I am no longer invisible.

"Hey, Maddox." A guy in a hockey jersey whacks Drew on the back. "Who's your friend?"

"You been holding out on us, Maddox?" another one says. I recognize him from the library. Ben-something.

Drew shakes his blond head, laughs. We keep moving.

A girl I've never seen before, with long brown hair and a tube top, gives me a dirty look. She mutters something to her curly-haired friend and they both crack up.

I get a twitch in my stomach but keep moving.

Now we are at the far end of the kitchen, and I find myself in front of a table full of bottles. There are about fifty of them and they are all different kinds, but it's as if my eyes are microscopes and all I can see is the brown one with the yellow-and-orange label. I try to breathe in, but there's only one smell, and it makes me want to hurl.

"So," Drew says, "what's your poison?"

I look at him. "Huh?"

"What do you like to drink? You a rum girl? Vodka? Peppermint schnapps? Kahlua?"

I look at the table again, and my heart is thumping in my chest. *Dr Pepper*, I think. *Juice.*

Drew is raising his eyebrows at me, waiting. I picture his face when I ask for a big glass of OJ.

"Anything," I say. "Anything but Jim Beam."

Drew nods. Smiles. And picks up three different bottles.

*   *   *

11:27 P.M.

I am on a bed, surrounded by coats, and I don't have a shirt on because someone has taken it off.

"Hey," a voice says. It is a voice with lips attached. Lips on my neck. Lips on my collarbone. Warm lips. Wet lips.

Drew.

"Hey," I say. I sound like I'm at the bottom of a well. "HeyDrew. AmIatthebottomofawell?"

"Huh?" Drew lifts his head.

My tongue feels like rubber. Why does my tongue feel like rubber? "Whydoesmytonguefeellikerubber?"

"Whoa." Drew laughs. "You're hammered."

I'm hammered, I think. *Hammered. Ha-mmerrrred.* I picture a giant hammer, silver with a red rubber handle. It's a funny thing to picture. Hilarious.

Lips on my ribs. Lips on my waist.

"Hey." I laugh. "Thattickles."

Lips on my belly.

"Hey."

Hay is for horses, but grass is much cheaper.

Hands on my belt. Hands on my zipper.

"Hey." I'm not laughing anymore.

"What?"

"Don'tdothat."

"Come on," Drew says. "You'll like it."

Hands on my belt loops, pulling down.

No, I think. *Nonononononononono.*

Hands on my underwear. White with blue flowers.

"No!"

Drew stops. "Come on, Sam."

I am shaking my head against the pillow. *Nononononono-nononono.*

"Don't tell me you've never done this before."

I shake my head. I have never done this before.

A long, low whistle. "You've been missing out, kid." Hands on my underwear. "Just relax."

You've been missing out, kid.

Hands on my underwear.

Kid.

"I'makid."

"Hmmm?" Hands pulling down.

"I'm a kid."

"What?" Hands stopping.

"I'm thirteen."

"*What?*" Drew jumps up like I've just touched him with a flaming-hot poker. "*What?*"

He is pulling up his pants. "*Thirteen?*"

"Jesus!" He is throwing coats.

Now he is swearing. At me. He is calling me names I've never even heard before.

And then, the worst thing happens.

He leaves.

CHAPTER TWENTY

I wake up in a different bed. My own.

I want to keep sleeping, but the sun outside my window has other ideas: *First blind her. Then jab her eyeballs with scorching-hot daggers.*

When I try to lift my head from the pillow, I find it is not my head anymore. It is the head of a two-ton elephant that has recently been clubbed.

Ohhhhhhh.

I try swallowing. Impossible. My tongue is wearing a wool sweater.

I lie perfectly still for a while. I don't try to remember last night. Or how I got here. Or anything. I just lie perfectly still, and breathe, and —

Oh. My. God.

Red plastic cup. "Looks like you could use a refill. . . . Hey, slow down there, tiger."

Drew.

Bed.

It's all coming back to me, the fragments of my night. Him leaving. Me crying. Me searching for my shirt. Me stumbling out of the bedroom, bumping straight into . . . straight into . . . who? A boy. A —

Andy Shaver. Bethany Shaver's brother.

"Heyyyy, Samannnntha. What are you doing here? Yo, wait. You can't leave yet. Have a drink."

Red plastic cup.

"Hey, wanna see my room?"

If I could go back in time, to that single moment, I could say, "I've made enough mistakes for tonight, Shaver, thanks." I could say, "Gee, Andy. That's sweet. But I'm a little impaired right now. Rain check?" Or, "Buzz off, bird butt." Anything but "okay."

Okay, Andy. And when we get there, will you shove me up against your dresser? Please? And mash all over me? That would be fantastic.

Sweaty hands. Dorito breath. Braces sharp against my mouth. Dark, dark room.

"Hey, you guys. Look who's here."

"Heyyyyy. Samannnntha."

Kyle Faulkner.

"No way."

Danny Harmon.

"Way."

Hard hands. Hard lips. Lizard tongues. Dorito breath. Braces sharp against my mouth. Dark, dark room. Until some-one opens the door and turns on the —

"Sammy?" It's my mother, sitting on the edge of my bed. "I want you to get dressed and come downstairs."

I try to speak, but all I can do is croak.

"Move now," my mother says. "Talk later."

*   *   *

Marybeth Martinelli brought me home.

When my mother tells me this, I can't believe it.

"Really?" I keep saying. "Marybeth Martinelli? Angie's sister? Are you sure?"

"I'm sure," she says.

"Positive?"

"Samantha." Now she's irritated.

"Sorry," I say. "It's just . . ."

"It's just what?"

I shake my head. "Nothing."

The truth is, I don't remember seeing Marybeth last night. Besides Juliet on the porch, and Hockey Helmet Guy, and Mean Tube Top Girl, and Drew, and Andy Shaver, mostly what I remember seeing is feet — a kaleidoscope of feet. Boots. Sneakers. Clogs. Platforms. Loafers. Roller skates. *Roller skates?* Yes. There were roller skates at some point, I am sure of it. Tan, with orange tassels.

"Sam?"

"Hmm?"

"*Sam!*"

"Ow!" I say. "You don't have to blow out my eardrums."

My mother passes me two pills. Tylenol.

"Take these," she orders. "For your head. And finish your juice. You're dehydrated."

"How do you —?" Well. I just stopped myself from asking the stupidest question in the universe. *How do you know what I need right now?*

The answer is so obvious I want to smack myself.

Right now, I am my father.

"Fine." I take the pills and drink the juice. Then I look around the kitchen. "Where's Luke?"

"At the Parkers'."

"Why?"

Instead of answering, my mother puts a plate in front of me. Toast with peanut butter.

"I know you don't want to eat right now," she says, "but you'll feel better with something in your stomach."

I shake my head. "I'm not hungry."

"Eat," she says.

"Fine."

The peanut butter sticks to the back of my mouth like glue, but I make myself choke it down because I don't have the energy to fight.

My mother sits and watches me. Her eyes are impossible to read. After I have finished my glue sandwich, she asks, "Do you need more juice?"

"No, thank you," I say. I fold my hands in my lap and wait for the inquisition to begin.

Tick, goes the clock. *Tick. Tick.*

Any second now, she will start firing questions at me. *Where were you last night? What were you thinking, Samantha? How could you have been so irresponsible?*

If she asks me what happened, I will tell her the truth. *Are you okay, Sammy?* she'll say.

No, Mom. Not really.

I wait.

And wait some more.

Nothing.

"Okay," I say finally. "How long am I grounded?"

My mother picks up the dishes and walks them over to the sink. She rinses them off and places them on the drying rack.

"Mom?"

I watch as she pats her hands with a dish towel, then begins wiping down the counter.

"*Mom!*"

I am practically yelling, but it doesn't make any difference. My mother has perfected the art of silent counter wiping, and it makes me want to bang my head against the table. I would do it, too, if my head weren't already killing me.

Finally, she turns around. "You want to know something funny?"

"I guess."

My mom gives a little laugh. "I miss your father's hangovers."

I look at her and open my mouth. But nothing comes out.

She walks over to the table and sits down next to me. "He didn't start drinking until senior year of college. Did you know that?"

I shake my head.

"It's true. Not a single drop. We'd be at a party and every-one would be drinking, and your dad would have a Coke."

"Why?"

"That was your dad," she says. "He was captain of the baseball team. Top of his class. All the girls wanted to date him. He was . . . that was just your dad."

She is looking down, but I can tell she is smiling. I can tell she is remembering someone I never knew, some guy she fell flat on her face for.

"So what happened?" I say.

My mother's smile goes back inside her now. "His father died that fall, and I think a part of your dad just shut down. Maybe it was anger, or maybe relief. It's a complicated thing, grief, when the person you're grieving is . . . complicated. Grandpa Gwynn was a big drinker, honey. And when he got drunk he got . . . pretty scary. Rough."

I have to whisper when I ask it. "Did he hit Dad?"

"Once." She holds the dish towel in both hands, twisting it. "Mostly he took it out on Nana. Not that she would ever admit it."

"Oh," I whisper.

Oh.

I have a hard time listening after that, but my mom keeps going: It was the Sigma Chi winter formal, the first time he drank. My father had three whiskey sours and serenaded her on the porch, in front of the entire baseball team. Later the two of them climbed to the top of the clock tower on the quad and rang the bell. Campus security came and yelled at them, but it was all worth it. That was the night they fell in love.

"We were so in love, Sammy. I can't even tell you. It was like . . . spontaneous combustion."

By this stage, I want to gag a little. There is only so much Cheez Whiz I can stomach. Still, she's on a roll, telling me about how my dad got accepted to architecture school and the baseball team was winning and every night was a party. Then, in the mornings, my dad would be too hungover to go to class, and she would make him coffee and juice and peanut butter toast, and put cold packs on his head until he felt better. After that, architecture school was the same routine: drinking sprees at night, my mom playing nurse in the morning.

"Uh-huh," I say, like I get it. But really, I am thinking, *Way to go, Martha Martyr. Way to be part of the problem.*

"Then I got pregnant with you, and we had to get married. And your dad stopped drinking. Just stopped. For five years."

She keeps going, but I don't hear what she's saying anymore. My ears are frozen on those five words she just said. *We had to get married.*

Wait. I was a mistake? My dad got wasted and knocked up my mom, and that's the story of my life? Oops! Bun in the oven! Better book the church!

I can't believe she is still talking.

He started drinking again when he joined the firm. Blah, blah, blah. *Late nights. Deadlines. Family to support.* Blah, blah, blah. *Stopped having hangovers altogether.* Blah, blah, blah. *Started worrying.* Blah, blah, blah. *First sign of physical addiction.* Blah, blah, blah.

I stand up and grab the juice jug. I start pouring juice all over the floor.

My mother stiffens. "Sam. What are you doing?"

"I don't know," I say. "I think I'm pouring juice on the floor."

"Honey, why?"

"I don't know!" I snap. "It was a *mistake*! It just *happened*!"

"Well, stop!"

Her voice is sharp, but I keep pouring, until the floor is an orange lake.

"Oops," I say, tossing the empty jug on the floor. "I guess I'll have to go get married now."

My mother looks confused at first. Then horrified. "Sammy, no. It wasn't like that."

But I don't give her time to explain. I run out the kitchen door, down the steps to the street, and I don't stop running until I get to the only place I want to be right now.

But it's Sunday.

The library is closed.

I knock and knock on the front door, for anyone. Miss Howe. A.J.K. Juliet. Even Shelving Guy.

But nobody comes.

CHAPTER TWENTY-ONE

On Monday, Angie is waiting by my locker. I am so relieved I could cry. If anyone will understand about a big fight with my mother, it's Angie. She and her mom are at each other's throats at least once a day.

I run over. "Angie. I really need to talk to you."

Angie turns to me, and her eyes are cool and narrow. "It's sooooo hard to find babysitters on Saturday night, isn't it?"

At first I don't get it. I even smile a little in my confusion.

"You can wipe that smirk off your face right now, Samantha. Marybeth told me everything. *Everything*." Her voice is frost cold — the coldest I've ever heard it. Even when she talks about Molly Katz, she is not this mean. This is pure hatred.

"Angie," I say.

She shakes her head. "No. You betrayed me."

"Let me explain."

"Don't bother." It's Tracey talking now, sidling up next to Angie. "You knew how she felt about Danny. What were you thinking, Sam? We wouldn't find out?"

Vanessa is right there behind Tracey. "If you didn't want to sleep over at my house, why didn't you just say so?" She doesn't sound angry, she sounds hurt. Which is almost worse.

"V. It's not like that, it's —"

"I really don't want to hear it right now, Sam."

"Okay," I say. I am nodding and biting my lip like crazy. "Okay."

I will not cry in the middle of the eighth-grade corridor. I will not cry in the middle of the eighth-grade corridor. I will not cry in the middle of the eighth-grade corridor.

The bell rings. I say "okay" a few more times like an idiot. Then I watch as my three best friends walk away.

*　　*　　*

Between first and second period, every eighth-grade girl goes to the locker room to watch Molly Katz stand on a trash can. Everyone except me. It's like I know what's coming. Three weeks ago I was Best Boobs. Today, I have been promoted.

Samantha Gwynn, Best One Night Stand.

By third period, I cannot believe what I am hearing about myself. The whole school is talking about it.

In dirt science, Jacob Mann looks at me and smirks. "Sounds like you had quite a weekend."

Just ask me what really happened, I want to say. *Ask, and I'll tell you the truth.*

But Jacob doesn't ask. No one does.

*　　*　　*

I didn't think the day could get worse, but apparently it can.

In gym class, Ms. Fish tells us to partner up. We're about to be tested. How many sit-ups can we do in three minutes?

She runs down her clipboard, barking out names. "Hunter and Jacobson. Fine and Hollander. Katz and Gwynn —"

Katz and Gwynn.

Of course.

Now I am flat on my back on the foul line, with Molly Katz holding my ankles. It is clear that she has sharpened her fingernails just for the occasion.

"One." Dig, dig, dig.

"Two." Dig, dig, dig.

"Three." Dig, dig, dig.

"Whore." Dig, dig —

Whaaat?

For a moment, I think I must have imagined it. I am hallucinating. Lack of oxygen to the brain.

I keep going. *Five. Six. Seven. Eight. Nine.*

"Slut."

Okay, that isn't even close to rhyming.

Don't do it, I tell myself. *Just ignore her.*

Molly Katz would eat me alive. I can picture myself walking down the hall, M.K. and her pack of she-wolves behind me, giving me flat tires, making the books fly out of my arms. It's what they do best. I've watched them do it a million times to Debbie Shultz, who's chubby, and to Tamara Manheim, who has zits and dresses like a guy. And every time I see it, I have to turn the other way because I can't stand to see the looks on those poor girls' faces. I have this little problem with people getting humiliated in public.

So I open my big mouth.

"Take your claws off my legs."

Oh, Sam.

"And shut your trap."

Way to think it through.

"Before I shut it for you."

Well. I have sealed my fate.

Molly Katz looks at me. She smiles so I can see every tooth. She doesn't say anything. She doesn't have to.

*   *   *

At lunch, Andy Shaver, Danny Harmon, and Kyle Faulkner get high fives. I get a chicken nugget in the head.

Go to your locker, I tell myself. *Go directly to your locker. Do not pass boys. Do not collect 200 insults.*

Okay, my locker has been redecorated, graffiti style. Some words I recognize, and some I think were made up just for me. I spend the rest of the lunch period trying to scrub it off, but it is Sharpie marker. Permanent.

*   *   *

By the time I make it to the library I am shaking all over. I pass the checkout desk, and Miss Howe says hello. She's never said hello to me before. It's the nicest thing anyone's said all day.

"Are you all right?" she asks.

I shake my head and keep walking.

I am not all right. I am all wrong, and I need to talk to someone, even if that someone is a person who doesn't exist except

134

between pages 32 and 33 of a book that hasn't been checked out in thirteen years.

Please let there be a note. Please let there be a note. Please let there be a note.

And there is.

Sam,

I was at the party. I know what happened. I'll bet school was a real treat today.

It's time we met.

Library parking lot, 8:30 tomorrow morning. I'll bring the doughnuts.

A.J.K.

CHAPTER TWENTY-TWO

Well, I am about to skip school for the first time ever. On my way out the door it occurs to me how easy this is. Why haven't I done it before? Just get dressed, throw on a backpack, and head to the mall. Or the zoo. You can spend the whole day relaxing because no one is there to make you do chin-ups or peg you with poultry.

But now I am a block from the library, frozen to the sidewalk. I don't know if I'm ready to meet A.J.K. just yet. I kind of like the note system. It works for me. Why would I risk walking into the parking lot and having A.J.K. take one look at me and think, *Wow. What a loser?*

I take a minute to converse with myself.

Get moving.

No.

Come on, Sam. What are you, chicken? Bock! Bock!

Yes.

Well, I don't care if you are. Go.

No.

Oh, that's just great, Samantha. Be a victim. Let the whole world walk right over you. Just stand there like a lump, feeling sorry for your —

Fine!

I can be very convincing when I need to be. I know how to push my buttons.

*   *   *

There is only one car in the parking lot — a lime-green station wagon.

The panic that I feel in this moment is big enough to swallow me whole, but I take a deep breath and keep walking.

The person sitting in that car knows me better than anyone else. She knows about my dad and about Luke's face. She knows why I change clothes in the stall instead of the locker room. She knows how furious I am with Charlie Parker, and how Drew's kisses make my stomach feel, and the list goes on forever.

Now I am picking up the pace. I am *running* toward the car. I am five feet away, four feet away, three feet —

The driver's door cracks open and a shoe steps out. An ugly shoe.

I look at it, confused.

Because I know this shoe.

I know it so well that now I feel like I've been shot full of bullets.

The door opens wider.

He is getting out. Standing up. Reaching out his hand for me to shake.

I can't breathe.

"Sam?"

Shelving Guy.

"Alexander Jessup Kaufman."

Looking straight at me. His eyes on my eyes.

"I'd like it if you'd call me Jesse, though."

I. Can't. Breathe.

"Are you okay? I thought you might be a little shocked at first. But I don't know . . . I thought we should meet, you know? I thought it was time."

I want to run, but my legs are cement blocks.

"I had an idea for today, of where we could go." Shelving Guy is smiling now. "It's kind of a surprise, though, so —"

"I am not. Going anywhere. With you."

"Sam."

I shake my head.

That's all I do. Shake, shake, shake. Also, I talk silently to my feet. *Please move. Please? Just move.* Finally, they listen.

Now I am sprinting across the parking lot. He is right there behind me. I can feel the bulk of him.

"Sam."

"No."

I keep running, past the fire station. The post office. The Subway. I run until my lungs burn, until my legs fail me again. Then I collapse on a bench, gasping for life. Shelving Guy is right there next to me.

"Why —" I puff, "are you — still — here?"

"Because," he says, "I think you could use a friend right now." He is not even winded, which is infuriating.

I lean back and close my eyes, feel my heart jackhammering in my chest. "Go — away."

"Sorry. Can't do it."

I don't respond at first. I am still trying to catch my breath. Plus, I need to come up with something. A real zinger to put him in his place.

"Listen, A.J.K.," I say, "I don't hang out with liars."

Shelving Guy looks at me. "I'm not a liar, Sam."

"Please. You told me you were a girl. If that's your idea of the truth, I'd like to hear —"

"I never told you I was a girl. You *assumed* I was a girl. I just never bothered to correct you."

I give a snort. "Lying by omission. Still a lie."

"Here —" He reaches into his jacket. "Documentation."

Now he is taking out his wallet, his driver's license, and I am trying not to look. But I am too curious.

I lean in and squint. *Alexander Jessup Kaufman. Height: 5-10. Weight: 160. Sex: M. Hair: nutso.* Then I notice something else.

"Michigan?" I say. "What is this, a fake?"

Shelving Guy shakes his head. "We just moved here in August. From Detroit." He slides the license back in his wallet. "And I hate the name Alexander. So I'm trying to, I don't know, start over. Reinvent myself." He shrugs, like he's embarrassed. "Jesse sounds better."

I look at him hard. "What's wrong with Alexander?"

Silence for a second.

Then, "It's my dad's name."

I nod. "Right. The mean, horrible tyrant forcing you to play soccer when you'd rather be playing Ado Annie opposite Tom Lombardo in the school —"

Wait.

"Is there really a Tom Lombardo?"

Jesse looks at me. "There's really a Tom Lombardo."

His eyes are so brown and steady that I might have to believe him.

"So you're, like . . ."

"Gay."

I nod slowly. "Okay."

What is a person supposed to do with this information? How is a person supposed to respond?

"So," I say, "your dad is, what? . . . Does he know?"

"He knows." Jesse makes a sound, like my earlier snort. "He just refuses to believe it's permanent. He thinks it's a *phase*. Curable by roundhouse kicks and slide tackles, you know?"

"Weird," I say.

"Yeah."

We sit for a minute, not saying anything.

Then I break the silence. "I've never met anyone gay before."

Jesse smiles. "Yes, you have."

"No, I haven't. You're the first one."

"I'm not. I promise you."

"How would you know?"

"I know."

Now I am starting to get peeved. "I don't think you are in a position to tell me who I have and have not met in my life."

Jesse smiles again. "Okay. I'm just telling you, ten percent of the population is gay. I'm not the only freak in this town."

I look at him. "I don't think you're a freak because you're gay."

"No?"

"No. I think you're a freak because of your hair. And your shoes."

*　　*　　*

It's 10:15 A.M. and instead of suffering through dirt science, I am riding shotgun in a lime-green station wagon, heading who knows where.

"How much longer?" I ask.

Jesse rolls his eyes. "We'll be there when we get there. This is a surprise, remember? Stop asking questions."

"Fine."

I make myself comfortable, kicking off my sneakers and stretching my feet out on the dashboard. The bottoms of my socks are pure black and probably stink, but I don't care. For once I am not trying to impress anyone.

A part of me is itching to ask more questions about the Gay Thing, but I don't. I will let him tell me in his own time. When he's ready. Plus, the silence is nice.

I wonder what everyone at school is doing right now. Did Angie and Tracey and V. notice I'm not there? Do they even care? Has a janitor cleaned off my locker yet? Or have Molly Katz and her graffiti mafia been making new and brilliant Sharpie additions in my absence? Jerks. Actually, I feel sorry for them. They can't come up with anything better to do than —

"How's everything at home?"

Jesse is glancing over at me.

"What?" I say.

"Your mom and Luke. How are they doing?"

"Great," I say. "Just great. My mother has forgotten how to breathe. And Luke has forgotten how to bounce. They're fantastic."

Jesse focuses on the road for a second, then back on me. "Sounds rough," he says. "How are you holding up?"

I shake my head. "I'm not really in the mood to talk about me."

"Okay," he says. "Want to talk about Drew Maddox?"

"Nope."

"The party?"

"No *way*."

"Okay."

Somehow, he knows not to push me. Which is like one of those crazy reverse psychology tricks that I hate so much. *No, really, Sam. You don't have to talk. You don't have to say a word.*

"I'm here," he adds. "If you change your mind."

"If you think that's going to get me to talk," I say, "you've got another think coming."

Jesse flips on his turn signal. "Okay."

"Okay."

I look out the window. I can't look at him when I do this. I have to look at something neutral, like trees. "You really want to talk about Saturday night?" I say. "Fine. Let's talk about Saturday night."

*   *   *

We are somewhere in New Hampshire, driving along back roads. On the highest hills, there's snow already. Jesse is steering one-handed, with the other hand dangling out the window, possibly getting frostbite. Once in a while he turns to look at me, smiling, and it's hard to believe that he and Shelving Guy are the same person. Here in the car, Mr. Down and Out is Mr. Cheerful and Confident. For some reason, this irks me.

"How come you never talked to me before?" I ask.

"What do you mean?"

"In the library. Whenever we ran into each other, you could barely look me in the eye."

"I could look you in the eye."

"No, you couldn't. You could look me in the belly button and mumble." I make my voice deep and low. "*This is the marine life section, you know.*"

Jesse shrugs. "Hey, I did what I had to do."

"To what?"

"To figure you out without you figuring me out."

I have no idea what he's talking about.

"Are you schizophrenic or something?" I ask.

"I don't think so. Let me check. *Jesse, are you schizophrenic? No, but Alexander is.*"

"Hardy har har."

I don't say anything for a minute, even though I have a

million questions. Like, *Are you happy?* And, *Do you wear your hair like that because you think it looks good or just to make your father mad?*

But instead I ask, "Why did you keep writing back?"

Jesse looks at the road for a moment, then at me. "Because you needed me to."

"Oh, so I'm like a charity case? That's just great. That's —"

"*And,*" he says loudly, interrupting, "because I wanted to. Because you're the bravest person I know."

I stare at him.

"You make me want to be . . . braver myself." He shrugs and his cheeks are red. "That sounds stupid, doesn't it?"

"No, it doesn't."

"Yeah, well. You need to close your eyes now."

"What?"

"We're almost there, and I don't want you to see yet, so close your eyes. Okay?"

"Fine."

I close my eyes. I even cover them with my fingers, that old grade school no-peeking thing.

"No peeking," Jesse says.

"I'm *not.*"

The car slows down, and I can feel my stomach flip-flopping all over the place.

Now there's a hand on my knee. "Remember what I said about being brave?" Jesse says.

"Yeah," I say.

"You can open your eyes."

The car is stopping. There is a wide expanse of lawn and a

tall brick building with a wrap-around porch. There are lots of windows and people walking around inside. There's a square white sign above the front door. I read it, and now I am about to fall over. Because there are no animals, no freshwater sources, and no trees to speak of anywhere.

*   *   *

I'm in a waiting room that looks like a living room. Fireplace, puffy chairs, a million books in bookcases — everything that's supposed to make you feel calm and centered, but I am not. I am freaking out more and more every second.

Here is Jesse on the couch next to me, flipping through an art book. There's not a single worry wrinkle on his face. Suddenly I want to pinch him.

"I can't believe you did this to me," I hiss.

"What?" he says, innocent as can be.

"*This*. I don't want to be here. I don't want to . . . never mind. I'm so mad at you I can't even talk."

"Hey." His hand is on my knee again. "It's okay to be scared."

"I'm *not*. I'm —"

"Sammy?"

I hear the voice and look up. There he is. My father, standing in the doorway. My father, wearing a blue checked shirt I've never seen before, and a new side part in his hair. Calling me Sammy.

Jesse leans over. "You okay?" he whispers.

I nod and I stand up.

I walk across the room to my dad, slowly, without saying a word. Then, I don't know how it happens, but I slap him across the face.

It's one of those moments that hang in the air, suspended.

Slap!

Silence.

Stillness.

Nothing except the bright red handprint on my dad's cheek.

I take a step back, but he moves faster. He doesn't say anything, he just hugs me, and now I'm crying. I'm snotting all over his blue checked shirt, and he's leading me out of the waiting room/living room onto the porch.

* * *

We sit in wicker chairs next to each other. It's freezing — too cold to be outside — but here we are anyway.

"Do you want my jacket?" my father asks, and I just shake my head. I can't speak. I'm scared to. Scared of what might come out of my mouth.

"I'm glad you're here, Sammy."

I don't respond. I don't even look at him. I keep my eyes on my fingernails, which need to be cut.

"Because I have something to tell you. And it's important . . . Sam? Will you look at me?"

I shake my head.

"Please?"

His voice sounds froggy and I can't stand it. But I won't look up.

"I don't know how to do this," he says. "I don't know how to —" He stops and I can hear the tears in his throat. It's in this moment I realize exactly what he's going to say.

Sammy. I'm an alcoholic.

I lift my head and look him square in the eye. "Yeah. You are."

*   *   *

On our way to the car, Jesse puts his arm around me and I let him. I am a little exhausted, so it helps to be propped up. But in a way I am buzzing, too. I just spent two hours talking to my father, which is pretty much a world record. My head is so full it might explode. Jesse doesn't know anything yet, but he is not pushing, either. That is what I'm beginning to love about him.

Now we are in the car, sitting cross-legged, facing each other.

"Tell me everything," Jesse says.

I smile.

"Or nothing. Either way. Tell me whatever you want."

"Well," I say, "my dad's an alcoholic. He admitted it, finally. It's the first time I heard him say it out loud."

Jesse nods. "That's big."

"Yeah."

We sit for a second in silence.

"He's got all these new friends now. All alcoholics and addicts. I got to meet some of them."

"Yeah?" Jesse says.

"Uh-huh. This one big black guy, Syrus, a cokehead but you wouldn't know it, he's my dad's Scrabble partner, took me aside and told me what a great guy my father is, and then he gave me the letter X. He just pressed it into my palm and whispered, 'I want you to have this.'"

Jesse stares at me. "Why X?"

"I don't know. A lot of points, I guess. Rare. Anyway —"

"Wait." He holds up his hand.

"What?"

"This is too good. I have doughnuts. How can we go on without doughnuts?" Jesse crawls into the backseat and rustles around for a while. Then he pops up with a white bag. His hair is weirder than ever, and there is this ridiculous demented grin on his face. "Honey-dipped or jelly?"

*　　*　　*

It is 9:00 at night by the time I make it home, and my mom is hyperventilating all over the kitchen. "Sammy!" she cries out when I walk in the door. "Where have you been?" She grabs hold of me and squeezes so hard my intestines wrap around my tonsils.

"I've been worried sick! I've been calling everywhere, but no one has seen you all day! I was this close to calling the police!"

"Relax," I say. "I was with Dad."

"*What?*"

"I went to see Dad today."

My mother stares at me. "How?"

"This guy drove me. Jesse. A friend of mine. . . . I met him at the library. He's . . . it's a really long story."

She pulls out a stool and pats it. "We've got all night."

I nod. All night in the kitchen with my mother could be torture. Or it could be the start of something.

After we are both sitting, I take a breath. "You know how I got drunk at that party?"

"Yes." My mom is looking at me, nodding.

"Well," I say.

Now she is frowning. "Sammy. Did something happen to you?"

"Yeah. A few things."

And then I open the floodgates.

CHAPTER TWENTY-THREE

I wake up with jumping beans in my stomach. The last place I want to go right now is school.

"It's only a half day today," my mom says at breakfast. "If you want to stay home you can. Help me bake pies."

I look at her blankly. "Pies."

"It's Thanksgiving tomorrow, honey."

Oh.

"We're going to the Parkers'? Remember?"

No.

My mother is using her softest voice and her warmest eyes. After everything I told her last night, she is now my best friend. "What do you say? Pumpkin? Apple? Whatever you want."

I shake my head. "I have to go to school."

"Are you sure?"

"I'm sure."

*　　*　　*

There's no one at my locker when I arrive, and I'm okay with that. Because I have a plan.

I gather my things and wait for the bell to ring. When it does, I walk with my head down directly to English class. I do the same thing for gym. Mouth shut, eyes on the floor. Just make it through the first few periods.

Not part of the plan: running smack into Charlie Parker.

"Hey," he says. "Watch it."

"Oh," I say. "You're talking to me now?"

"No. I just think you should watch where you're going before you get a concussion."

"I think *you* should watch where *you're* going."

Charlie rolls his eyes. "Good one."

We stand there in the hallway, staring at each other.

"So," he says low, "is it true?"

"Is what true?"

"What everyone's saying. About you."

I keep staring at him.

"Is it?" he says.

"You tell me."

"How can I tell you? I wasn't there."

I shake my head, disgusted.

"*See?*" Charlie says. Now he's smiling.

"See *what?*"

"See what it feels like not to be believed?" He backs away down the hall, fists in the air, champion of the world.

I give him my dirtiest look. It's all I have for comebacks today.

*   *   *

Now I am late for dirt science. It is possible to sneak past Mr. Ryder, but there is no avoiding Jacob Mann.

"Where were you yesterday?" he says. "Recovering from your *wild weekend*?"

"Stuff it, Jacob," I tell him.

"Oooooooh."

Mr. Ryder is giving us the death stare. It is either pretend to be fascinated by his rock lecture, or detention.

I take out a piece of paper and start copying off the board.

Igneous rocks (a.k.a. fire rocks): two types
  1) underground — formed when the melted rock, called magma

Well, I am so bored I might have to scream out loud. Or change my note-taking strategy.

You know that time capsule you guys did last year?

I angle my paper toward Jacob and kick him under the table. He kicks me back.

Who's the numbskull who stole my bra and charged everyone a buck to see it?

Jacob grins. He is so amused.

I am so not.

YOU REALLY WANT TO KNOW? he writes.

Do you really want to live until 4th period?

Jacob grins some more.

I hold up my sharpened pencil like a dagger, but he is having too much fun messing with me to mind. He might actually get stabbed.

"Fine," I whisper. "Don't tell me. I don't really care."

"Surrrre you don't."

"Anyway, I know it was Charlie Parker."

"Parker? That chicken —"

"Mister *Mann*." Mr. Ryder's voice booms like a cannon. "Do you have something to share with the class?"

"Yes, sir, I do," Jacob says. "May I stand?"

Mr. Ryder glares at him.

"Okay. I was about to confess to Samantha here that *I* am the scoundrel who stole her bra last year and charged everyone a buck to see it. And for that I am truly —" Jacob begins to break down in mock anguish. "Truly —"

"Enough!" Mr. Ryder roars.

He tries to direct our attention back to rocks, but it's too late. The whole class is cracking up. And now the bell is ringing.

I gather my books. "You'd better not be lying to me."

Jacob grabs my hand and clamps it to his chin. "Look at this face, Sam. Look at it. Would this face lie?"

*   *   *

School is over and I have only one thing to do: Find Vanessa. She is where I knew she would be, at Angie's locker, with Tracey. But I have to wait until she's alone because Angie is still too mad to be reasoned with, and Tracey acts whatever way Angie does.

There is some spying involved. I find an excellent spot behind the door in the teachers' lounge. And wait.

Finally, Vanessa is saying her good-byes. She is giving out Thanksgiving hugs. She is walking out the door to the buses.

Jackpot.

I follow her out, ordering my stomach to unknot itself. This is *Vanessa*, one of the kindest, gentlest people I know. Not a mean hair on her head. The best place to start.

I take my place beside her in the bus line. "Hey, V."

She turns to me. "Hey."

No smile, but no silent treatment, either. So far, so good.

"Taking the bus?" I ask.

"Yeah." Vanessa adjusts her backpack on her shoulders. "My mom had to go pick up the turkey. Which is like four hundred miles away on some organic farm, so I'm stuck with no ride."

"At least she's using a real bird," I say. "Remember in fifth grade when she made the Tofurkey and we all had to pretend it was the best thing ever?"

Vanessa giggles.

I am *in*.

"So, are you still having everyone over on Saturday? Like always?"

Vanessa stops smiling and looks at the ground. "I don't know, Sam," she says. "Angie and Tracey are still pretty mad."

"So I'm not invited? Is that what you're saying?"

Vanessa lifts her head a bit, and her face is miserable.

Gotcha.

"I just don't think it's a good idea," she says. "You know? Until things . . . cool off a little?"

I nod. My stomach is getting tighter and tighter. But I make myself say the words. "I need to come on Saturday. I just do."

She's silent for a moment, like she doesn't know what to say. Then she looks at me. "Why?"

"Why?"

"Why do you need to come this time when last time you felt just fine about blowing us off for some party?"

"That's why I need to come. I need to explain a few things."

Vanessa is shaking her head. "I don't know, Sam."

"What, you can't make a decision without consulting Angie? Is that it?"

Her face changes, gets a little hard. "That's not fair and you know it."

Backpedal, backpedal, backpedal.

"You're right," I tell her. "That wasn't fair. I'm sorry."

She nods. "Accepted."

Vanessa's bus is pulling up and the driver is opening the door. He is red-faced and pissy looking — the kind that won't wait for long.

Vanessa looks at me. "I have to go."

"Okay," I say. But I want to grab her by the backpack. Because she hasn't said what I need her to say, which is *Sure, Sam, you can come on Saturday and tell us everything and then we will all forgive you and be friends again and eat leftover turkey sandwiches and pecan pie straight out of the pan at two in the morning.*

I watch her step onto the bus. I watch her walk to the back, where she takes a seat next to Debbie Shultz, who nobody else will sit with.

Now the bus is pulling away and I am running along next to it, waving wildly. I am dorking out big-time, but I don't care.

Finally, Debbie Shultz notices and pulls down the window. "What?" she yells.

"Tell Vanessa I'm coming, anyway!"

Debbie turns away from the window for a second. Then back again. "She says you're crazy!"

Well, maybe I am. And maybe I will just have to take that as an invitation for Saturday night because the bus is going too fast now, and I can't keep up.

*　　*　　*

For the first time in the history of modern whaling, I am on the phone with A.J.K.

"I can't stop thinking about it," he says. "I'm obsessed."

"Maybe he just picked it out of the box," I say. "Randomly. And it happened to be an X."

"No. There's got to be some hidden meaning."

"Like what?"

"Like that drug. Ecstasy."

"But Syrus is a cokehead," I say. "It's an entirely different thing."

"How do you know?"

"Health class. Stimulants? Hallucinogens? You know."

"Okay. How about X-rated?"

"What? You think he's a perv?"

"Maybe."

"Great," I say. "Now I'm going to be freaked out all night. Thanks a lot, Jesse."

*　*　*

"The only other thing I can think of is X-ray," he says during phone call #2. "And *X marks the spot.*"

"Hmmm. What about kiss? Like you'd sign at the bottom of a letter. X-o-x-o-x-o."

"Nah. Too cutesy. Syrus doesn't sound like the kind of guy who would x-o-x-o somebody."

"Maybe not," I say.

"I need to know! How can I be thankful for anything tomorrow without knowing the Meaning of the X? How can I go on living?"

I think about this. "Doughnuts?"

Jesse laughs. And I have no choice but to stay on the phone for another hour.

CHAPTER TWENTY-FOUR

It is a weird thing to have Thanksgiving at your ex-best friend's house, especially now that you realize he is not the bra-stealing money-grubber you thought he was. It is hard to know how to proceed.

It's even weirder to have Thanksgiving when your own father is not there to carve the turkey.

Mr. Parker is doing it all right: one plate for white meat, one plate for dark. Perfect slices and neat stacks, which is how it is supposed to be, I guess. Not like my father would do, with everything thrown together in a big messy mountain, everyone having to dig around for what they want. He never used an electric carver, either. It was one of those things — he always used the same old knife with the cracked handle and he always said, *Time to butcher the bird!* My mother would make the gravy, but she would call it *gravity*, and it would be lumpy, and she would always burn the biscuits. It wasn't the best meal, but really it wasn't the worst, either, because my dad would make a toast saying he was thankful for us, his family. Then he would take a big slug of red wine, of course. But so would my mother, and at least they were using the fancy glasses from their wedding day.

Here at the Parkers' we say grace, which I have never

understood. First we hold hands and stare at our plates. Peas: tiny, green boulders. Turkey slices: rafts floating on a gravy river. Then Mrs. Parker thanks our Heavenly Father for the bounty we are about to receive, but the only Father I can picture is my dad, and I am wondering what kind of bounty he is receiving right now. Probably it is like school lunch in the cafeteria, some kind of mystery meat in scary sauce. And stewed prunes for dessert.

After we are allowed to eat, Luke gets down from his chair and runs over to me. He doesn't say anything — he just climbs up on my lap and stays there. His stitches are gone and he isn't a giant bruise anymore. But the scar on his cheek is pink and naked looking, and the haircut my mother gave him makes everything worse. Now his ears stick out.

I hold him tight and eat nothing but mashed potatoes, trying to decide why I feel so strange and mixed up, why I can't just be thankful like I am supposed to be.

I think, what if my dad was here right now, would he be falling face-first into the cranberry mold? Or maybe this time, by some miracle, would he say, "No, thank you" when the wine came around? And have milk instead? I would like to believe it's possible, in some alternate Thanksgiving universe.

Now we are excused from the table for an hour before the pie. It is the cue for me and Charlie to talk and we are both pretending it's not. But I can feel he wants to and probably he can feel I do, too. Faye and the Barbies have kidnapped Luke, and the mothers are in the kitchen doing dishes, and Mr. Parker has gone to watch the ball game. At the table, it's two ex-best friends, alone.

We are having another one of our staring contests. Which I could win easily. It's with this knowledge that I open my mouth.

"Well," I say, "I had a little chat with Jacob Mann yesterday."

Charlie raises one eyebrow.

I try to raise one eyebrow back at him, but I can't. Whenever I try to raise one, I raise two, which makes me look surprised, the opposite of cool. It's the same thing with winking. I always end up blinking.

"And?" Charlie says.

"And I know he's the one who took my bra, okay? Not you."

"And?"

"And I know he made twenty-seven dollars and you wouldn't pay a cent. You walked away from the whole thing."

"And?"

Well, now he is pushing his luck.

"And *what*?" I ask.

Charlie looks me full in the face like a teacher. "Don't you have something else you want to say to me?"

"What?" I say. "*I'm sorry?*"

"Is that a question?"

Oh, he is so infuriating. "I'm sorry. Okay? Is that what you want me to say? I'm sorry I didn't believe you at first. But I believe you now."

Charlie nods. "Good."

"Good," I say, and it takes every bit of strength in my body to keep the snottiness out of my voice.

*　　*　　*

Well, this is it. The new start of Charlie and me, because we are once again in the fort in his backyard, eating pie. We are wearing big puffy coats, and I am wishing we had gloves, too, because my fingers are about to break right off from the cold. But the pie is good, blueberry. And there is ice cream on top, which at least is not melting.

"So," Charlie says, "are you going to tell me what happened on Saturday night or what?"

I look out the fort window at the yard. Except for Charlie's house, it is pure black out there. I can choose to talk or not talk. It's all up to me.

"Fine," I say. "But turn off the flashlight."

"Okay."

The fort goes dark and I start talking.

"I didn't want to go in Andy Shaver's room. But I was already pretty tipsy and then he gave me something else to drink. 'Send it, Sam,' he said, which means drink it really fast, and I did. Then he pulled me in and shut the door, and I was really dizzy and I couldn't see, and Danny and Kyle were there, too."

Charlie doesn't say anything, but I can feel him right there with me, a warm lump.

"They all started mashing on me at once, and I couldn't stop them because they were pinning me against the dresser. I couldn't even breathe because their tongues were in my mouth."

I stop for a second, and Charlie says quietly, "Then what?"

"Then someone came in and turned on the light and yelled, *Get off her.*"

"Who?"

"I don't know. I really can't remember. Some friend of Angie's sister, I guess."

"Martinelli?"

"Yeah. And they let me go. That's all. I know everyone's saying I did stuff to them, but I didn't. And they didn't do anything to me, either. Just kissing. Which was still pretty bad because I had no choice."

In this exact moment it hits me. "That's what it's like," I say.

"What's like?"

"Being drunk. It makes you stupid." I think about being in the bed with Drew, his hands on my bare skin. That's a whole other part of my night that Charlie doesn't need to hear about. "It makes you do things you would never do in a million years."

"So why did you drink?" Charlie says.

"I don't know. I guess I wanted to see what it was like."

I can feel Charlie standing up. "I'm going to pummel those guys."

Pummel? Who says *pummel*?

"What guys?" I say.

"Shaver. And Harmon and Faulkner."

"That's a little dramatic, don't you think? Pummeling?"

"No." Charlie flicks on the flashlight and I can see his face, scowling. "I don't care how drunk you were, or how drunk they were. They had no right to do that to you, do you hear me?"

"Yeah." Of course I hear him. I have ears.

We walk across the yard together, toward the house. "Do you think if people do stupid things when they're wasted they should ever be forgiven?" I ask.

"I don't know. I guess it depends on the situation." He

stops to open the door, looks at me. "Your dad's coming home soon, huh?"

I nod. "Nine days."

Nine days, eight hours, and sixteen minutes.

But who's counting?

*   *   *

When we get home, Mom and I sit on the edge of Luke's bed, watching him sleep. He looks so small, lying there. There's blueberry pie on his chin, and his bangs are sticking straight up.

"That is a really bad haircut," I say. "Promise me you'll never do that to him again."

My mother makes her *shhh*ing noise and points to the door.

I don't want to leave Luke, but I get up and follow her into the bedroom and flop down next to her.

"What did the doctor say about the scar?" I ask her.

"We're supposed to wait and see how it looks in a month. How it's healing. Then we'll decide how to proceed."

"Does Dad know?" I flip over onto my stomach and start playing with the edge of the pillowcase. "Are you, you know, talking to him and stuff?"

"Yes," my mother says. "We've spoken a few times."

"And? Is he sorry?"

"Of *course*."

I look at her. There is that *Oh, Sam* expression on her face.

"Your father loves you and Luke very much."

"You always say that. *Your father loves you very much.* If he loves us so much, why can't he change? Answer me that."

She thinks about this for a moment.

"It's not that simple, Sam. I used to think his drinking was a choice, but it's not. I wish I'd tried to get help sooner, but there were always excuses, justifications. It wasn't really a *problem*. He could stop *anytime he wanted*. He was getting promotions at work. I'd look at him and think, *Okay. He's fine....*"

"Mom," I cut in. "He's not fine."

My mother reaches over and brushes a piece of hair out of my face. "I know."

I look down at the pillow again. There are so many questions in my head. *Is my dad going to lose his job? Is my mom going to have to go back to work? And if she does, what would she do? She's never done anything. Bag groceries at the Shop-Co? And what if my dad never stops drinking? What if he hits Luke again? What if he hits me? Will they get a divorce? Then what? Or, what if he* does *stop drinking? What will he be like? Who will he be? How will we know how to act?*

"Mom?" I say.

"Hmm?"

"What did I get from him?"

She looks at me. "What do you mean?"

"I know what I got from you. Your hair. And we can both put our feet behind our head. And we love Chinese food. And puzzles. And when we sneeze, it's always five times in a row. Exactly. You know?"

My mom nods, taking it in.

"But what did I get from Dad?"

"Oh, honey."

"I'm serious."

"Well." She settles into the bed, propping herself up on one elbow. "In college, even though he was an architecture major, your dad took a lot of math classes. For *fun*. I always thought he was crazy, but he just really loved math. He was great at it. Like you. And . . . when he's concentrating hard, he sticks out his tongue a little bit, like this —" She stops to show me. "Just the way you do. And . . . is this the sort of stuff you mean?"

I nod, and she keeps going.

"You have the same . . . I don't know. Capacity for tenderness. The same essential goodness, you know? Remember that dead bird you found in the backyard when you were eight? The funeral you held for it?"

I roll my eyes, but at the same time I'm blushing.

"Do you know what your daddy did once?" she asks.

I shake my head.

"It was winter and we were walking downtown by the shopping center, and there was a woman with nothing on but a T-shirt. Clearly homeless. And your dad took off his coat and gave it to her. His brand-new ski jacket."

"He did not."

"Yes, he did."

"Was he wasted out of his mind?"

My mother looks at me. For a second I think she's going to bawl me out, but instead she says softly, "No, honey, he wasn't. That was a good day."

We stay on my parents' bed for a long time, while my mom tells me things I never knew about my dad.

I lie on his pillow and close my eyes and listen. Because there's so much I don't know.

CHAPTER TWENTY-FIVE

Well, I'm almost at Vanessa's house. I can't believe I'm about to tell my friends what I'm about to tell them, because I've kept it to myself for so long. But I'm ready.

Now I'm standing on the porch and ringing the bell. Even though it's freezing out, my hands are so sweaty I have to wipe them on my jeans.

Mr. Barton answers the door. He gives me a big hug, saying, "Sam! We missed you last weekend!" He hopes I'm hungry because there is enough leftover turkey to feed an army.

Two seconds later, I am sitting at the butcher-block table, facing the firing squad. Angie, Tracey, and Vanessa are staring me down. Tracey has her arms crossed over her chest. Angie's eyes are hard.

They are not going to make this easy.

"Hey," I say.

Even though no one says *hey* back, I keep going. "I'm sorry about last weekend. And about lying to you guys. And, Angie, I'm sorry about Danny. I'll tell you the truth about that in a minute, but it's not really what I came here to say. And don't worry — when I'm done, I'm not planning on staying over. I didn't even bring pajamas."

Everyone's eyes are on me. I want to look down at the table, but I make my head stay up.

"I came here to tell you about my dad and how he drinks all the time. I've always tried to hide it from you guys. Because I was afraid of what you would think. And now he's in this rehab place because he got really drunk and hit Luke, and he's coming home in a week, and I don't know what's going to happen. I know it's no excuse for last weekend, but I just needed you to know."

Vanessa has moved over next to me. Her arm is around my shoulders, and I am crying a little.

"Angie," she orders, "get the tissues. Tracey, get the turkey."

She uses her pajama sleeve to wipe my face. "You know in *Raquel's Promise*, when Raquel finds her birth certificate and realizes she was adopted and everything she knew up until that point was a sham? And she thinks her life is over and has that total breakdown, and she calls Wilhelm in hysterics, and in two seconds he is right there by her side?"

"Yeah." I say. "So?"

"So. We're Wilhelm."

* * *

In spite of everything I am at Vanessa's the next morning, wearing her mom's cat nightgown. Things are almost back to normal. Almost.

Angie is still punishing me a little — making a point to sit next to Tracey at breakfast, rolling her eyes ever so slightly when I ask her to pass the syrup. I don't call her on it because I know she will come around eventually. Once, in sixth grade, when she asked me to cut her hair, I gave her a bilevel and she hated it. It took her three weeks to forgive me.

"So," Tracey says, "what are you going to do about that Drew guy?"

I shrug.

"Are you, like, ever going to talk to him again?"

"I don't know," I say. Because I don't. Funny how you can be so embarrassed about something, and mad, and still when you think about that person you get the old tingle in your belly.

I take a bite of waffle and realize I'm tired of talking. I am done with it. No more baring my soul about my dad or boys or anything else for today. I will eat waffles and drink cocoa. Later, I will go home and climb into bed and just lie there. Until I figure out what to do next.

* * *

Midnight, and I am having a snack at the kitchen table. The silence of the house wraps me like a quilt. The light from the street makes long shadows on the linoleum. It is spooky, but not.

Tonight is popcorn with whatever I can find for toppings: pistachios, rainbow sprinkles, Nerds. This may be my best invention ever, but I can't make myself eat. I can't stop looking at the doorway. It's crazy, I know, but I am expecting my dad to appear any second, wearing his striped bathrobe and one sock. His hair everywhere. Holding a big brown bottle.

That's when it hits me, what I should do.

My feet start moving before I can tell them where to go: the cupboard to the left of the sink.

I reach past the bleach and the sponges and the garbage bags until I feel it. Bottle #1. This is the one he uses for his morning coffee — I know for a fact because I've seen him do it a million times.

Well. Not anymore.

*   *   *

It takes an hour. The final stop is my parents' bedroom, where I am on my hands and knees in the closet with a flashlight. I check every single pocket. Every shoe. In his slippers I find two tiny bottles — mouse size. Ha!

The bag is so heavy now I can barely lift it. Somehow I manage to heave it over my shoulder, Santa Claus style. Santa Claus, the sick and twisted version.

I am stumbling and clanking all over the place, but my mother doesn't make a peep. I stand next to her bed and stare.

"Mom," I say.

No answer.

"*Mom.*"

Nothing.

"I'm going to take all of these bottles outside and chuck them at something hard, okay?"

Okay, then. The sleeping pills on her bedside table are coming with me. The more, the merrier.

CHAPTER TWENTY-SIX

"Knees up, Frances!"

I only slept for two hours last night. It defies logic that I should be able to move an inch. And yet —

"Frances! Knees up!"

And yet I manage to keep running.

Molly Katz is not in school today. Everyone is talking about her weekend. Apparently she was on a movie date with Greg Vaughn and reached over for some Milk Duds and farted. She tried to pass it off as a squeaky clog, but there was no hiding the air pollution. Now she is *Molly La Pew*. Her locker has been toilet-papered. Even her friends are stinky by association. The eighth-grade boys are having a field day.

I am yesterday's news.

"Three more laps!" Ms. Fish yells in my ear. She is wearing sweatbands on her wrists like she thinks she's Wonder Woman.

My heart thuds in my chest.

"Pump your arms! Pump!"

My right shoulder aches, a memento of last night.

I stand in the middle of the garden, nodding at the garage, until I'm ready to wind up and let one fly.

Okay, I was never much of a pitcher in Little League, but last night, I have to say, I was spectacular.

Bottles soar. Glass shatters. One minute the air smells like leaves, the next minute it is the most disgusting smell in the world and you have to breathe through your mouth. But you don't stop.

"Pump!"

I pump, and I lift my knees, and every muscle in my body is screaming at me, but I don't stop. I keep going.

Two and a half laps left.

Two and a quarter.

One.

The whistle blasts and I collapse against the wall.

Ms. Fish walks over with her stopwatch.

"Six minutes, forty-two seconds," she barks. "Good hustle, Frances."

I raise an eyebrow at her. Well, actually, two eyebrows, but who cares.

"The name," I say, "is *Sam*."

*　　*　　*

The library is buzzing tonight. The jock table is a rainbow of baseball caps — every color imaginable, except for green.

I've been watching the doorway for twenty minutes, and so far no Drew. Which means one of two things: a) he fell into a manhole on his way to the library, or b) he's off mashing with his new, eighteen-year-old girlfriend.

Either way, I wore mascara for nothing.

Looking around the room, you have to wonder, who will Drew Maddox take to the water fountain next? Long Black

Braid? Fuzzy Boots? Eyebrow Ring? Of course, there's always Juliet. Juliet, who probably carries five cartons of cigarettes around in her backpack. Maybe she is Drew's type exactly — his one true love. And if she is, am I supposed to feel sorry for her or hate her?

I can't decide.

When I get to the stacks, Jesse is waiting.

"Looking for a good book on whales?" I quip.

"Oh," he says in mock surprise. "Are you an expert?"

"As a matter of fact, I am. May I recommend to you *The History of Modern Whaling* by Tønnessen? It's faaabulous."

Jesse grins.

I grin.

We are the two biggest dorks in the library.

"I brought you something," he says.

"It doesn't have anything to do with turkey, does it? Because I'm *done* with turkey."

"No turkey," he says, and hands me a bunch of books.

Books that have absolutely nothing to do with whales.

Dear Kids of Alcoholics

Everything You Need to Know About an Alcoholic Parent

Alateen: A Day at a Time

"Oh," I say, nodding. "Uh-huh."

"I thought you might find them helpful," Jesse says. "Before your dad comes home. You know?"

"Yeah, well." I find a spot between sea turtles and seaweed and shove them all onto the shelf. "I didn't ask for your help."

Jesse stares at me. "You're kidding, right?"

"Do I sound like I'm kidding?"

"You abso*lute*ly asked for my help."

"No, I didn't."

"Yes. You did."

"I did not!"

"Okay," Jesse says. "I didn't want to do this, but . . ."

Now he is reaching into his back pocket, pulling out a square of paper, unfolding it. Clearing his throat.

"What?" I say. "You prepared a speech?"

Jesse holds up a hand for silence. "'Here is the deal,'" he says. "'First of all, my parents. They are a total mess. My dad is what you would call a big drinker which really equals a big —'"

Oh. My. God. I make a grab for the paper, but Jesse side-steps out of my way.

"'If you ever have time between high school activities to tell me what you would do in my shoes —'"

"Stop that!" I say.

"Stop what?" he asks, innocent as can be.

"Reading *me* to *me*."

He considers this for a minute. Then says, "'I think if you write back, you would be a big *help*.'"

I take another lunge but he dodges me again.

He is unstoppable. "'And maybe I could be a help to you in some way, too. With baking tips, for example'. . . . Wait a second." He looks at me. "Sam. You promised me baking tips. Where are my baking tips? After everything I've done for you . . .'"

I don't want to smile, but I do. "You. Are such. A freak. I can't believe you carry my notes around in your back pocket."

"I don't," he says. "Normally. I just knew how you would react, so I needed to be prepared."

"Oh, I see. You know everything about me now?"

"Not everything. But I'm getting there."

This makes me roll my eyes a little.

He grabs the books off the shelf and hands them to me *again*. "Just take these home, okay? You don't even have to read them. Just sleep with them under your pillow."

There are so many things I could say to him right now. Sarcastic things, snotty things. But in this one moment a thought slams into my head. Whatever Jesse is doing, no matter how infuriating, he is being a friend.

"You're a real pain, you know that?" I say.

He grins. "Takes one to know one."

"Do you know who you sound like?" I say. "Charlie Parker. And your hair is sticking up at a ridiculous angle."

"Those are compliments, right?" Now he is grabbing my backpack and filling it up with alcoholic-dad books. And I am letting him.

It's a funny thing, friendship. One minute a person is driving you crazy, making you want to shake them, and the next minute you realize what a crappy place the world would be without them in it.

While Jesse zips up my backpack, I think about the next step. One of these mornings we will go for breakfast and I will buy the doughnuts. Honey-dipped, jelly, Boston cream, whatever. We will make small talk for a while, and then I will ask him about his dad. And about Tom Lombardo. Just in case he needs someone to talk to. I will be that someone.

CHAPTER TWENTY-SEVEN

Well, today is the day.

Sunday, 6:14 A.M., while all normal families are sleeping, mine is in the car, driving along back roads in the middle of nowhere, staring out the window. At 9:00 we will pick up my father. Then we will bring him home.

Last night, instead of staying over at Vanessa's, everyone came to my house. For the first time in history, I laid out the sleeping bags on my own living room floor. I made the snacks. I set up the Ouija board and waited for the doorbell to ring so I could greet my guests like a proper hostess.

Hello and welcome.

Hello and welcome.

Hello and welcome.

If you are ever picking your father up from rehab in the morning, some advice: Take advantage. It may be your last possible chance to host a slumber party.

After my mom and Nana and Luke went to bed, we snuck out into the backyard. The moon was big and round in the sky and our breath came out in white puffs. I showed everyone the broken glass all over the ground, and Tracey said, "You're just going to leave it there?" And I said, "Yeah. For now."

"No offense," Angie said, "but what if he just buys more bottles?"

"Well," I said, "I'll smash those, too."

At first, I was mad. Because what does Angie know? Nothing. What does anyone know? Their fathers are normal.

Later, I couldn't sleep. I couldn't stop picturing my dad reaching into one of his hiding places, feeling around for a bottle, finding nothing. Who knows what he would do next. I'm afraid to picture it because what if Angie is right? What if he just buys more bottles?

"Sammy?" my mother says now.

"What?" I ask.

"How're you doing, honey?"

Her eyes look for me in the rearview mirror. A little makeup on them today. Nana did it for her before we left. Mascara. Brown shadow. It looks weird.

"Honey?"

"I'm fine," I say. Then, "My stomach hurts a little."

"Should we pull over?" she asks. "Do you want a Tums?"

"No. I'll be okay."

I look at Luke, asleep in his car seat. It makes me feel better, in a way, looking at him. His face is calm and soft. "I'm just . . . I don't know," I say. "Nervous, I guess."

"I know," my mom says. There is a moment of quiet in the car, a long moment, and then she speaks so low I can barely hear her. "I'm nervous, too."

"Yeah," I say.

There's one thing I could use right now, and that's tarot cards. Or a crystal ball. Something. A gypsy woman with bangles on her arms to swoop down into the car and say, "Now, don't you be nervous. He's going to get better, your dad, and when he's better, everything else will be, too."

It sounds crazy, I know. And I know that the notes I left all over the house may not make an ounce of difference, even though I used my best stationery and took my time to fold in a special way.

Think before you drink.

Choose booze, you lose.

Don't be a blockhead, try juice instead.

Jim Beam's a bum. Here's some gum.

Why puke when you could hug Luke?

I know, I know, I know — I'm not going to win any poetry contests. But at least I've tried, and at least he will find something if he goes looking for bottles. And I do believe that finding something is better than nothing.

I lean over and kiss Luke's cheek. The scar is still there, a fat pink snake from his nose to his ear. I trace it lightly with my finger. I bury my nose in his neck and breathe in the sweet, milky warmth of him.

Then I sit back and look out the window, see that it is starting to snow.

Well, whattaya know?

Maybe, if there is enough, we'll build a snowman later. Maybe my mom will bring out the hot chocolate and my dad will put Luke up on his shoulders, taller than everyone — tall enough to stick on the corncob pipe and the button eyes and the carrot nose.

"How does it look, buddy?" he will say.

And Luke will yell, "Great!"

Maybe, at that moment, someone will walk by and think we're a normal, happy family.

And maybe, for that moment, we will be.

ALCOHOLISM RESOURCES
FOR KIDS AND TEENS

HOTLINES

(Remember that these calls won't cost you anything
because they have an area code of "800" or "888."
Just be sure to dial the "1" first.)

Alateen
1-800-344-2666

National Association for Children of Alcoholics
1-888-554-COAS (2627)
8:30 a.m. – 5 p.m. (EST), M – F

National Youth Crisis Hotline
1-800-448-4663

National Runaway Switchboard
1-800-621-4000

Drug and Alcohol Resource Center
1-800-784-6776 (Provides help and information about any drug
or alcohol related subject. If you or someone you know has a
drug addiction or alcohol abuse problem, calling this number is
a great place to start.)

WEB SITES

Alanon/Alateen
www.al-anon.alateen.org

"For over fifty years, Al-Anon (which includes Alateen for younger members) has been offering hope and help to families and friends of alcoholics. It is estimated that each alcoholic affects the lives of at least four other people . . . alcoholism is truly a family disease. No matter what relationship you have with an alcoholic, whether they are still drinking or not, all who have been affected by someone else's drinking can find solutions that lead to serenity in the Al-Anon/Alateen fellowship."

e-mail: wso@al-anon.org

National Association for Children of Alcoholics
www.nacoa.org

"A place where you can: learn how alcohol and other drugs hurt everyone in a family; learn how to feel safer and less stressed out; find new ways to deal with hassles at home; find hope, even if your parents don't change."

e-mail: nacoa@nacoa.org

Children of Alcoholics Foundation
www.coaf.org

"Children of alcoholics and other substance abusers are at risk. But with help and support, they can be taught to cope with their parent's problems, and break the intergenerational cycle of this disease."

BOOKS

Alateen—A Day at a Time from the Al-Anon Family Group Headquarters, Inc. This book offers a thought for every day.

Alateen—Hope for Children of Alcoholics from the Al-Anon Family Group Headquarters, Inc. This book explains what Al-Anon is all about.

An Elephant in the Living Room, The Children's Book by M. H. Typpo and J.M. Hastings. This book has a program to help young people deal with the problems of living with a problem drinker or drug-abusing parent or sibling.

The Children's Place. By Jerry Moe, M.A. and Ross Ziegler, M.D. This book includes artwork and letters of children of alcoholics.

Living Today in Alateen from the Al-Anon Family Group Headquarters, Inc. This book is a collection of personal sharings from Alateen members around the world. There is a different page for each day of the year.

Kids' Power Too: Words To Grow By by Cathey Brown, Betty LaPorte, and Jerry Moe. This book offers a thought for every day.

My Dad Loves Me, My Dad Has a Disease by Claudia Black. A workbook that helps young people learn about themselves, their feelings, and the disease of addiction in their families through art therapy. Children between the ages of six and fourteen share what it is like for them to live in a family with alcoholism or drug addiction.

Something's Wrong in My House by Katherine Leiner. A book about domestic violence and alcoholism and how it affects children. The book deals with the universal feelings of fear, anger, and hopelessness and looks for ways to help people cope.

Think of Wind by Catherine Mercury. A story about how alcoholism impacts families.

Have You Ever Been a Child? (Hints for Children & Adults) by Leslie Gebhart. Simple illustrations with hope-filled messages give inspiration to children of all ages.